Spidey Legs
❧Lana❧

Tessa LaRock

Cover design by Mark Reimann.

ISBN 978-0-9821075-6-0

Printed in the United States of America

Acknowledgements:

I want to thank my son and my daughter,
Brant and Amanda,
for all the wonderful times
we have had together.
I am very proud to be your mother.

Chapter 1

LYNN'S TRAILER PARK

The heated sun blazed at nearly 98 degrees and Evan irritably swiped an arm across his dampened forehead. He ran alongside a broken-down wooden fence that enclosed one of many run-down modular homes in the surrounding trailer park. Several dogs barked in the not-too-far-off distance and the smell of trash and someone burning food was thick in the air. Lana was just ahead and he needed to help her, protect her from harm at any cost.

"Run Lana! Run!" he shouted to her. She awkwardly scrambled beneath a fence where she was trying to elude four men who were making their way from one backyard to another in the attempt to catch her.

"I can't!" she cried, as she fell to the ground entangled in a mass of silken webs and spider legs. "I can't!"

"Shit! I knew this would happen," Evan muttered as he hurriedly scaled another fence then two over-turned garbage cans. He finally reached her. Gathering Lana's slender body into his arms, he ducked a large open fishnet which raced in his direction and landed just before his feet.

Lana screamed.

Evan's heart banged within his chest as he leapt a plastic big-wheel, darted behind a metal shed and made a dash for the clearing.

"I'm sorry," she exclaimed through trembling lips. "I'm sorry." Her enormous dark eyes were wet with tears and she wiped them away with a closed fist. And, though she was seventeen, she reminded Evan of a little girl.

"Save it till we get outta' here." His feet pounded along the dry earth and he blinked back the sweat that stung his flashing dark eyes. "We hav'ta hide! I don't know how much longer I can run in this heat."

Evan glanced back at the four men. Three were the build of barrels and one was long and scraggly, similar to that of a scarecrow. He knew they would never be able to keep up; they were huffing and puffing twice what he was, even though he himself was over 100 years old. What worried him most were the rifles they carried— bullets were faster than anything Evan's legs could ever put out, even if he did transform to his arachnid form and use all eight.

"Grab the kid!" one of the men shouted.

"He's too damn fast," came a reply.

"Then, shoot their asses!"

"Shit!" Evan's heart jumped and he briefly glanced

down at Lana who stared up at him through terrified eyes. *Ignorant fools,* he thought. *This isn't over yet.*

Evan ran from the trailer park and into an open cornfield. The field had long since been cut and was dried to brittle stalks and dirt.

Breaking through a patch of heavy brush, he arrived on the edge of the precipice which overlooked the rushing waters of the Haim River. He came to a screeching halt and looked down. The river, surrounded by cutting boulders and sharp rocks, was a good 200 foot drop from where he stood. Its water moved forcefully, pushing its way through the valley and running toward Brenton Forest which was located just two miles from their home.

Knowing he would have to double back and circle around, he turned to head in another direction. Suddenly, the tall scraggly man burst through the thicket of brush and weeds.

Evan spun back around facing the edge of the cliff and mentally prepared himself to jump.

"They're over here!" The man, resembling a scarecrow, wheezed slightly and bent to take a breath.

A gruff voice shouted back, "I know, I got 'em!"

"Hold on, Lana."

Suddenly, a shot rang out and Evan pitched forward. Pain rushed through his entire body at lightening speed and he gasped for air.

The massive force sent him and Lana careening over the edge.

Chapter 2

BEAR MOUNTAIN
3 MONTHS EARLIER

"**Martin**, where are you going?" Barb Patterson, thirty-two, with dirty-blonde hair and green eyes, looked up from the book she was reading and asked her husband as he suddenly brought the small camper to a halt. "I thought we were going to Bear Mountain to camp."

"Bear Mountain's closed, dear. Or didn't you see the sign back there." Martin Patterson, in his late-thirties, dark-haired and dark-eyed, glanced at his wife through his sunglasses. "I have to turn around."

The camper jarred and jolted as he backed the cumbersome vehicle onto a small knoll and pulled back out onto the dirt road. "I'm not sure where to go now."

Lana sat up and rubbed her eyes. She had fallen asleep during the long ride from their home while her younger brother, Samuel, lay sprawled across the seat beside her. She looked down to see his dirty bare foot shoved in her lap.

"Ewww!" She shoved his foot away. "Samuel, keep your feet to yourself!" The young boy, just turning eleven, with green eyes and sandy blonde hair, yawned and stretched. He clutched his favorite action figure and turned on his side to go back to sleep.

Lana turned her attention from her brother to the mountainous area around them. Thick pine trees lined each side of the road and layered the valley far below. They blanketed the mountains, covering them completely except for their peaks which disappeared into the clouds.

Lana loved the outdoors: hiking, the fresh air, biking, and swimming in the beautiful crystal-clear lake. She wasn't a very athletic girl or rough-and-tumble like her little brother; however, she loved the quiet and peacefulness.

She and her family had frequented Bear Mountain in the past few years, giving her father the much needed vacation he desired from his sixty-hour-a-week job.

Her mother and father would find a quiet place to park the camper; then, after they had found a great spot to set up, she and Samuel would go hunting for firewood. Their father would then set up the barbeque grill while their mother would search through the cupboards and many bags selecting the perfect assortment of foods for supper.

The camper came to a sudden halt and stirred Lana from her thoughts. She looked at her parent's, wondering what was so intently drawing their attention. They each stared toward an old deserted camping entrance which disappeared into a junction of pines. A rusted chain lay broken across the road and the entrance was partially grown up with shrub and vegetation.

Martin Patterson pushed his sunglasses up to rest above his dark brows which were knitted together. "Whaddaya' make of this, hon?" He then glanced at his watch. "It's getting late and we need to find someplace to park and set up camp. If we doubled back to Edgar Falls now, it'd be almost 7:30 by the time we'd get there. And, I don't wanna' be making camp in the dark." Martin looked over at his wife who was trying to read the rusted sign attached to the chain which was partially covered by dirt and weeds.

"I don't know." She pushed her sunglasses back. "There's a *No Trespassing* sign; but, we can't go wondering around the mountains all night trying to find someplace to park. Maybe it'd be okay for just one night. Then we'll head back to Edgar Falls in the morning. We just won't get the grill out tonight and I'll just have to make up a few sandwiches and a salad. Then, we can grill out tomorrow."

"Okay, then it's settled. We'll camp here at *Camp Forbidden*," Martin jested. "Then we'll head back to Edgar Falls in the morning." He turned the camper onto the weed covered road and slowly drove through the archway of hovering pines.

They entered the abandoned campsite. It was

overgrown with thistles, milkweed and foxtail which scraped along the bottom of the vehicle as they headed toward a slightly clear patch of stone parking area. The area surrounding the old campsite was vast and wide. It opened to a magnificent view of the far-off valley and rushing river below. It was breathtaking.

"Wow! This is really neat!" Lana nudged her brother. "Look, Samuel."

Samuel reluctantly sat up and was closely observing his father's every move from behind his father's seat. He and his father were close; and Samuel admired the man in every way.

"Dad, where you goin'?"

"I know this isn't our regular spot, Samuel, but it's nice and we really need to set up camp before dark." He spoke to himself, "I wonder why they've closed these grounds? It's beautiful here."

"Alright, Dad—whatever you say." Ignoring his father's latest remark and before the camper was even at a standstill, he opened his door and jumped from the camper. His feet hit the ground running and he was off to the water.

"Samuel..." their mother cried as he ran toward the river. She quickly rolled down her window. "You'd better be careful down there!"

Waving a hand of dismissal, Samuel raced down the

side of the hill.

Barb shook her head and muttered to herself, "That boy."

"Aren't you glad I'm a girl, Mom?" Lana asked. She leaned forward and gave her mother a kiss on the cheek.

"Yes I am." Her mother warmly smiled at her and winked.

Evening was readily approaching and night was slowly creeping along the mountain's peak. It brought everything beneath the bulky pines to a darkened pitch.

Lana and her brother sat quietly on a huge boulder which protruded out over the rushing river below. Both, full from supper and a box of cupcakes, lazily tossed loose stones into the water while their parents sat just outside the camper reading—Barb, a favorite romance novel and Martin, a New York Times magazine.

"I think this place is really cool," Samuel stated. He grabbed for a firefly that flickered just before his face. "I wish we'd stay here all week." He glanced back at his parents, ready to argue the point that they should stay. Then, thinking better of it, he looked to his sister for support.

"I don't know," Lana shrugged. "It is really neat here, and it was great that Mom and Dad let us set up the tent to sleep outside; but there must've been a reason why the area was closed off." Lana stood to her feet. "Welp, I'm gonna' go ta' bed now. We're leaving early in the morning and I wanna' go down near the river and get a couple of those tadpoles for my fish tank before we leave. They're really cool—they're blue."

Lana dreamt she was swimming in the crystal clear waters beneath the mountain and Samuel was getting ready to jump in and join her. Suddenly, she was jarred from her sleep; and though the tent was zipped tight to keep any bugs or animals out, she was certain she had felt something crawling along her leg. She quickly opened her eyes.

The inside of the two-man tent was dark as shadows hovered before her face and she attempted to adjust her eyes. She was positive she had felt something, so she reached for the flashlight. The thing invading their tent suddenly crawled across her foot. She screamed.

"What is it?" Samuel kicked the tangled blanket from his legs and awkwardly scrambled to his feet.

"Something's in the tent!" Lana stumbled forward then backward as she groped at air to keep her balance and also avoid whatever was in the tent with them. "Where's the stupid flashlight?"

"I don't know! It's probably under the sleeping bags!" Samuel, not nearly as fearful of creepy-crawly things as his sister, quickly dropped to his knees and searched for it.

"Oww!" he suddenly cried out. "Something just bit me!" He jumped to his feet and he and Lana cracked heads.

Tears rushed to Lana's eyes as pain flashed white within her head. "Samuel! Watch what you're doin'!" She rubbed her forehead. "*Mommmm!*"

The door to the camper banged open and light spilled from inside. Barb, dressed in robe and flip-flops, hastened out into the dark to the small tent which sat just feet away.

"What's the matter?" She hurriedly unzipped the dual-zipper. "I heard you screaming."

Lana pushed past her brother and rushed from the tent. "There's something in the tent! It just bit Samuel!"

"Are you guys okay?" Their father appeared at the open camper door in boxers and a t-shirt. He ran a hand through his mussed hair and yawned.

"*No*," Lana cried. "Something's in the tent, Dad. I don't wanna' sleep out here!"

"Come on, honey." Her mother placed an arm around her quivering shoulders and the other around Samuel. "You two come on inside. I wanna' check out that bite on your brother anyway, and put some antiseptic on it. Hopefully, it was a mosquito, and especially, not a spider..."

The kitchen and bathroom were arranged in the center of the camper. Lana and her brother slept on one bunk in the camper while her parents slept on another larger one at the opposite end. Lana had been having a terrible nightmare; it consisted of deadly spiders crawling along her entire body and something continuously poking at her shoulder. It was Samuel. Her eyes slowly opened. "What's wrong?" she asked him, thankful for being woken up.

"Sis, I don't feel so good," Samuel's body trembled beneath the blankets and the heat blazed from his skin to hers. Her body was also covered in sweat and she was chilled. She ran an arm across her forehead; it was also hot.

"I'll get Mom."

Lana slid from beneath the covers and stood to her feet. Her pajamas clung to her dampened body and twinges of pain rushed throughout her head. She took two steps in the direction of her parents, reeled around dizzily and flopped like a fish across a table of utensils. Everything, including herself, crashed to the camper floor. The last thing Lana remembered hearing was the thunderous sound of metal clanging, and Samuel screaming for their mother.

Chapter 3

BRANT MILITARY LABORATORY

"**Doctor** Leanette, what do you think we have here?" the lab assistant asked as she handed the young female physician a syringe. As the doctor flicked the syringe with her index finger, the tiny bubbles in the golden liquid disappeared. With assured accuracy, she swiftly injected the needle into Samuel's thigh, and though he was sleeping, he winced in pain.

"I'm almost certain they came in contact with something in Sector 8. I thought that area had been closed off. The military sure does a lousy job of keeping civilians out of there."

The female assistant took the empty syringe from the doctor and laid it on the metal tray along with several other syringes and instruments for collecting tissue samples.

"This will keep the fever under control. And as for any mutative transformation or cell modification, we'll have to keep these two under observation." Doctor Leanette removed her dark rimmed glasses and cleaned them with the corner of her white lab coat. "You say these two are brother and sister?" She examined Samuel's palm then laid his hand on the examination table next to him. She then proceeded to take Lana's hand and do the same with hers. "Where are the parents? And, where were they when all this occurred?"

The young assistant retrieved a clipboard that was attached to the end of Lana's bed where Lana lay sleeping. She flipped through the papers to the information on the children's parents. "They're Barbara and Martin Patterson; and the two children are Lana and Samuel Patterson— ages seventeen and eleven. The parents stated that they had no contact or symptoms of any kind. However, the boy was bitten on his hand which is evidenced by the large welt, and the girl, Lana, was unknowingly bit on the ankle. Both had symptoms of elevated fever and severe muscle ache and pain.

The parents had assumed the boy's bite to be a regular bug bite until the girl awoke in the middle of the night with an extremely high fever and passed out trying to awaken them. In the process, she hit her head on the corner of a table in their camper—that's where the abrasion on her forehead came from."

Doctor Leanette pushed back Lana's bangs and examined the blue and purple knot formed just above the teenage girl's right eyebrow. "This is the least of this girl's problems." Then, she examined the bite mark on Lana's ankle.

"Have the parents sent to my office. I need to meet with them. The last thing we need is this whole mess blowing up in our faces. We're supposed to be professionals for crying-out-loud. Damn incompetence.

DOCTOR LEANETTE HORN'S OFFICE

Barbara Patterson sat with her purse on her lap. She fidgeted with the handle on the bag as she listened to the words the doctor spoke in reference to her children and the dire situation at hand. She felt as if she had stumbled into a nightmare which wasn't allowing her to awake and she turned to her husband to see his reaction.

"Mr. Patterson, Mrs. Patterson, didn't you take notice to the signs that were posted at the entrance? Also, there was a chain across the road. Wouldn't that have given you any indication that the area was off limits?"

"No. It wouldn't, doctor." Martin Patterson stated. "Especially when the sign was lying in the dirt and the chain was rusted and broken. If there was something in the vicinity which was detrimental to my children or anyone else's welfare, shouldn't there have been a better security system in place? This *is* a military screw-up isn't it?"

The doctor sat forward in her chair and folded her

hands on her desk. She was quiet for a brief moment, then spoke.

"Yes, you're right—this is a military matter. And, unfortunately for you, this is where it must remain, *here*, within this facility. So, this leads us to the problem of what we are going to do with you and your children. You will have to remain here."

"Now, wait just one doggone minute. What are you trying to say—that we can't leave?" Lana's father stood to his feet and motioned for his wife to follow. "We're taking our children to a real hospital."

"Mr. Patterson—" the doctor reached beneath her desk and pushed a security button. Two heavily armed guards appeared through her office door. "If you'll remember, the hospital was instructed to bring the children here. We need to run tests and they cannot give your children the proper medical attention that will be needed. So please, sit down and listen to what I have to say."

Barb Patterson stepped toward the doctor's desk and the guards quickly stepped forward. The doctor raised her hand as a sign to wait.

"What kind of tests are you talking about, Doctor Horn?" Barb's voice cracked slightly. "I want to know exactly why our children were brought here and not kept at Mercy General. What were they bitten by anyway? And, what were you people doing out there that would cause a bug bite to be so dangerous? I want some answers!"

Lana slowly opened her eyes to a raging headache and a throbbing pain along her spine. She looked around the dimly-lit room. It wasn't an ordinary hospital room like she and her brother had first been taken to. It was more like a lab, like one she had seen on television. She glanced to her right to see Samuel lying on the table next to her. He lay on his back quietly sleeping beneath a thin white blanket. And, though the room was quiet, every movement of a blanket, puff of Samuel's air, or batting of a lash, seemed to echo in the hollowness of her auditory perception. Searching through her muddled mind, she attempted to recall what had happened and how they had gotten there. Everything seemed a blur and all she could remember was awakening in a cold sweat in the camper, the sound of her brother screaming and briefly opening her eyes at a hospital. Something was very wrong.

Lana tried to move her arms and legs, however, she was strapped to the metal table and was unable to budge. Terror ripped through her pounding heart and, *"Mom?"* came as barely a whisper through her choking throat. Tears formed in hers eyes and she blinked at their coming.

"Samuel," she quietly called to her brother. He didn't stir.

"Samuel!" His name echoed along the white, empty walls. "Samuel, wake up!" His eyelids fluttered slightly and he moaned.

"What's the matter, Lana?" He tried to move his arms and legs. "Hey, why am I tied down?" His wide eyes scanned the room. "Where are we? And, where are Mom and Dad?"

"I don't know." Lana was unable to hold back the flood of tears that now ran along her trembling cheeks. *"Mom! Dad!"*

A door quickly opened and an African-American man in a long white lab coat appeared. He was big and bald, possibly as old as Lana's father, and he looked agitated, maybe even slightly angry. Lana closed her eyes, pretending to sleep—Samuel did the same.

The man's footsteps echoed along the barren walls matching the rhythm of his wheezing breaths as he made his way to Samuel's side. Clearing his throat, the man then surprisingly spoke, his voice thundered within the room.

"I know you two are awake. I could see you both in the monitor just outside this room. My name is Isaac and I will be observing the progression of your bodies into their next formation. You will be monitored very closely every step of the way."

"What?" Samuel cried out as his eyes flew open. "We're gonna' *transform*? Wow! That is way cool!"

"No it's not, Samuel!" Lana, now ignoring the man's presence, opened her eyes and glared at her brother. "We're real people, not anime characters or superheroes! I don't wanna' transform into anything, I wanna' go home. You don't know what we'd transform into anyway; it could be a cockroach. Think a little bit, brother!"

Samuel looked back at his sister. "Aw, Lana, you always were a worrywart. Even a cockroach would be cool—they're nearly indestructible!"

"That's gross!" Lana laid her head back and closed her eyes again. Anger at her brother's stupidity surpassing the fear that just previously had her in tears. Samuel was known for doing that—getting on her nerves.

Isaac moved to Lana's side and gently held her petite wrist between two extra-large fingers; he checked her pulse. All the while, he mildly chuckled at the banter between brother and sister, which reminded him of his childhood bickering with his own siblings.

He smiled. "No. No-one's turning into a cockroach— hopefully not anyway. Though, a few of the others brought here could have passed for—

"*What?*" Lana and Samuel chimed in, interrupting the man's explanation. "There are others who were held here? Why?"

The man retrieved the chart at the end of Lana's bed and jotted some notes on it. "I've said too much already.

I will leave the explaining to Doctor Horn. She will be in to visit you soon."

The air seemed to slightly chill as Doctor Horn entered the room and turned on the overhead fluorescent lights. Samuel's wide, green eyes blinked at the intensity of the lighting while both he and Lana observed the woman's every move. She approached swiftly and professionally, as her white coat snapped with crispness and her heels struck the tiled floor. A hint of vanilla soap and medicine wafted about the room. The doctor went to Samuel's bedside first.

The woman's voice rang with authority as she spoke. "I am Doctor Horn, Doctor Leanette Horn. You two may refer to me as Doctor Horn." She glanced briefly at the chart she had removed from beneath her arm. "I see you are Samuel, age eleven; and you are…" she looked at Lana. Their eyes met and Lana quickly looked away… "Lana, age seventeen." She laid the chart upon a nearby table and pulled back Samuel's cover to reveal his upper body to the waist. She briefly examined his torso then promptly replaced his blanket then did the same to check his legs. Reaching into her pocket, she removed a small tape recorder and spoke into it. "Subject, male, eleven years of age, exhibits no signs of abnormality." She switched the recorder off, slipped it back into her pocket, then went to Lana's bedside. Lana kept her eyes on the bright lights above, refusing to make eye contact.

"Miss Lana..." Doctor Horn peeked beneath Lana's cover. Lana's pajamas had been removed and all she wore was her underwear. Lana blushed and quickly turned her head.

"I have just recently met with your parents, and after I examine you both, I will allow them to see you." She pulled a pair of surgical gloves from her pocket and slipped them on.

The doctor's cold fingers ran along Lana's stomach then briefly came to a stop. She closely examined something to the right of Lana's navel then she covered Lana's torso with the blanket and pulled back the cover to her waist. "Hmm...very interesting. Isaac, I need your assistance," she spoke into the monitor in the far corner of the room. The door quickly opened and the man appeared.

"Yes, Miss Horn."

"Isaac, I need you to turn the girl onto her stomach."

"Yes, Miss, right away."

He pulled a set of keys from his pocket and swiftly unlocked Lana's straps. Quickly and gently she was turned on her stomach and the shackles reattached. She was somewhat grateful for she was beginning to feel uncomfortable being in one position for so long. It felt like she was lying on a mound of hoses making her back extremely sore. It was strange.

Samuel watched through wide eyes—fear and curiosity for his sister's condition drew his undivided attention. He watched the man carefully roll Lana over, make her somewhat comfortable, then lock the thick steel bands holding her wrists and ankles.

"Oh my God," slipped from Samuel's lips. He caught his breath and excitedly blurted, *"No way, Lana!* You have spider legs growing out your back!"

"What?" Lana attempted to twist her head to see. "That's not funny, Samuel!"

"No. I'm not being stupid or anything. You *really* do!"

Eight, long, dark figures were nestled tightly against Lana's skin. Each was hair-covered and thin—like spider legs. They were entangled with one another and twitched every so often.

"Oh my God! What is that?" Lana twisted around trying to see the eight strange figures that were pressed tight to her back. "Let me go! Get them off me!"

The spider-like legs, seeming to react to Lana's emotions, began to come alive. The more she cried out in panic the more they twitched and flicked at the air. They began to whip about wildly, while silver strands of webbing crept from her stomach and slivered along her body. The webbing was coming from the rust-colored hourglass-shaped marking to the right of her navel.

The tape recorder appeared and was immediately switched on. Doctor Leanette spoke very slowly and distinctly as she observed the scene before her.

"Lana Patterson, age…" She glanced at the chart "…seventeen. Female Caucasian appears to be in good physical and mental health. We'll call her 01150." She paused, watching as Lana squirmed and the fine, almost-clear threading materialized from the mark on her stomach. "Subject has a rust-colored marking approximately two and three quarters inches in diameter, three inches in proximity to the right side of her navel. Marking is hourglass-shaped and produces a silky, thread-like substance compared to that of webbing from an arachnid. Subject 01150 is unable to control threading which wraps itself around its host.

Subject 01150 also has eight appendages growing from her lower vertebrate which uniformly blend into the hip and pelvis area—similar to subject number 01131—Evan, last name Labonte. Each is approximately three feet in length and two inches in width. They are blackish-brown in color and are covered in tiny black hairs. Until now, they have remained dormant and appear to have reacted to the girl's emotional state—also very similar to 01131's response."

Doctor Horn then switched the tape recorder back to off and slipped it into her pocket. She, along with Isaac and Samuel, watched as the silk quickly wrapped itself around the eight legs securing them to Lana's back.

"Isaac, I want you to get the exact measurements of the eight legs. Then, I want the mark, where the webbing is being produced, to be measured and photos taken. Record the girl's vitals and the other information I need, and then bring the results to my office."

The doctor turned and began to walk toward the door to leave. Then, she remarked over her shoulder. "Oh, and please place the girl on her back; for when I have the parents come in I want the appendages secured beneath her and unseen. And, also, give each of the children a substantial dose of morphine. That should retract the girl's legs if she's anything like 01131—or, at least, calm them down. I don't want too much being said by either of them, or too much being seen."

Chapter 4

Lana stared blindly at the white ceiling above her. The humiliation and fear she had felt an hour ago was now suppressed by the heavy dose of medication Isaac had given her. She could briefly remember him smiling at her and Samuel as he had given them each the injection. It was all so strange.

She hadn't felt a thing as the large gentle hands had measured, turned her body, taken her vitals then covered her. She was completely numb. It was as if she had been observing the whole procedure through someone else's eyes—eyes which spilled tears that had long since dried against her cheeks. She wanted to go home.

"Sam-uel?" Her voice sounded foreign to her ears. It was the medication. Not only was it making her numb, but it was also distorting her perception. She no longer could feel the mass of legs pressing against her back, maybe they were gone.

There was no reply from Samuel; she thought he must be sleeping.

Time passed and their mother appeared within a sluggish haze of Lana's mind. Her face was drawn, displaying a lack of sleep and stress that Lana had never seen before. She blinked her eyes, unsure if she was dreaming as her mother called out her name.

"Mom?" came as barely a whisper as tears rolled down Lana's cheeks.

"Lana, honey." Her mother grabbed her hand in an attempt to remain brave, however, failing miserably.

Tears flowed from both their eyes as Barb awkwardly tried to embrace her daughter—the restraints held Lana steadfast to her bed.

"I don't understand why my children have to be strapped to their beds." She glared through angry wet eyes at Doctor Horn and Isaac. "They're being treated like dogs!"

"I agree," Martin Patterson added. "I want these shackles removed and my children taken to a *real* hospital! Plus, you have them so drugged up they can't even sit up or move their heads! What the hell's goin' on?"

Samuel awoke at the sound of his father's angered voice. "Dad—" He could hardly be heard. "Remember what you always told me…slow to anger." His faint smile faded and he closed his eyes.

"I know, son." Martin Patterson took his son's limp hand, as he, normally being a gentle man, now fought the raging anger building inside him.

"Mr. and Mrs. Patterson, I told you this wouldn't be easy. I explained all of this in my office. Your children are now a potential danger, not only to themselves, but also to others. The restraints and medication are only to slow the effects of the toxin that is running through their bodies. By getting them riled up, you'll only be adding to the rapidity of their negative state." Doctor Horn grabbed his arm. "Mr. Patterson...please."

Martin Patterson looked to his wife then into the eyes of the woman before him.

"No." He swiftly reached into his jeans pocket and produced a large switchblade knife. It was one he used for filleting fish. Grabbing the doctor from behind, he rapidly flicked open the blade and pressed it against the side of her throat. Isaac stood ready to make a move, however unsure at this point what it would be.

"*Martin?*" Barb Patterson gasped, "What are you doing?"

"I'm taking control of the situation, dear. I'm taking the kids outta' here."

"But, honey...

"Quiet, Barb." His hand shook and he attempted to conceal the fear surging inside him. "You—Isaac, remove those shackles from my children."

Isaac glanced at the doctor in uncertainty. She nodded her head, reluctantly agreeing to the children's release. "Mr. Patterson, you're making a big mistake."

"Just shut up! Taking my children away from here

could never be a mistake!"

Isaac unlatched Lana and Samuel's restraints. Barb Patterson rapidly grabbed them both to her and blubbered I love yous.

"Barb, there isn't time for that now. Can you carry Samuel?"

"I'll try." Wiping the back of her arm across her eyes, she wrapped the blanket around her son and lifted him onto her shoulder. Fortunately, Samuel was thin, just hitting eighty-five pounds; and though Barb was petite, she was strong for her size. Working out at the gym three days a week had almost guaranteed that.

"Mr. Patterson, where will you go? You won't be able to get past the security guards outside the complex. They won't hesitate to shoot either you or your wife."

"Just shut up! I'm getting my children outta' here." With one arm, he awkwardly hoisted Lana, who was also fortunately small for her size, over his shoulder. "You and your organization are responsible for this. We'll see what the local authorities have to say about it." He motioned his wife toward the door as he followed behind with the doctor at knifepoint. "Oh, and if your assistant tries to follow us, I will gut you like a pig."

"Mr. Patterson." Her voice was condescending. "I doubt you could harm anyone."

The tip of the blade suddenly jabbed a little deeper

into the flesh of her neck. "Don't put it past me. When it comes to my family, I'd do anything to protect them... including killing you."

The five headed out into the hallway. As soon as the door closed behind them, Isaac hit the security button. Several alarms sounded throughout the building.

"Which way outta' here, Doc?" Martin shouted above the blaring sirens.

She grudgingly answered, "Follow the corridor to the end, turn right, then go through two double doors. The exit is on your left."

Martin pressed the knife snuggly to the doctor's skin. "Now, tell me how to get outta' here, where the guards *aren't* watching."

Doctor Horn shot him a nasty look. "Alright. When you get to the end of this corridor, go left. Then, take the stairs down to the basement. There's a way out through there that isn't being guarded. You're going to regret this, Mr. Patterson."

"No, Doctor—I'm afraid you are."

The sound of blaring sirens vibrated within Lana's ears and the realization of what was happening brought her mind into a semi alert state. "Dad? Where are we going?" He was racing down a flight of stairs. "Where's Mom and Samuel?" Her father's breathing was heavy and his body was tense.

"Don't worry, honey. We're getting you and Samuel outta' here."

They burst through a set of double-doors and out into the night. The blaring security sirens were sending armed officers racing in every direction.

"Martin, what do we do now?" Barb stated, out of breath. "I don't know how much longer I can carry Samuel."

"Where's our vehicle, doctor?" Martin's hand shook as he jabbed the doctor with the knife. A trickle of blood ran down her neck.

"Ugh!" she cried out. "It's to the left by the side gate!"

Martin's mind galloped in a thousand directions. "Distract them, Doc, so we can get to our vehicle."

"What?"

"Take that damn tape recorder you have in your pocket and say into it, *Help me, I'm over here*. Then turn the volume all the way up and hand it to my wife. Honey, you toss it as hard as you can in the opposite direction of the camper, toward that clump of weeds over there. Then, we'll run."

"Okay." Barb's eyes were large as saucers as she numbly nodded her head.

The doctor reluctantly did as she was told—the

recorder was tossed and they ran.

"Come on, honey!" Martin shouted, as they rounded the corner of the building to where the camper was parked deep within the shadows. He awkwardly dug the camper keys out of his pocket, unlocked the side door and quickly laid Lana on the camper floor. Samuel was placed beside her.

"Mom?" Lana's voice quivered.

"It'll be okay, honey." Barb briefly patted Lana's leg, then the door was slammed closed.

"Get down on the ground!" Martin suddenly growled at the doctor. "I said to get down!" Lana heard the doctor grunt and then there was silence. Her parent's footsteps echoed in her ears as her mother and father raced around the vehicle, jumped into the front seats and slammed their doors. Her father then started the vehicle and sped out of the compound.

Her parent's hearts pounded like thunder within their chests, and Samuel's being closer was the big bass drum. Lana wondered as to how she was able to hear such a thing. Closing her eyes, she listened closely to the various other sounds surrounding them.

Gunshots rang loudly within her ears as they ricocheted off the camper's siding and Lana winced with each one. Her eardrums thrummed with the screeching commotion as several vehicles raced along behind them and her father cursed.

She and Samuel were tossed about the small camper as it sped along the mountain road and hugged each curve, searching the dark for a means of escape. Items flew freely about the back, from groceries and kitchen utensils, to luggage and Samuel's toys. They crashed against the walls and burst upon the floor—Samuel was nearly pelted with a Hamilton blender.

"Hang on Samuel!" Lana cried out amongst the calamity as she grabbed for the support bar near the door. All of a sudden, the camper missed a sharp turn in the road and for a brief moment became airborne. Then, wrapping itself around a tree, it burst into two sections.

Chapter 5

Lana painfully opened her eyes to the blackened night and was surprised to find that she could clearly see everything that surrounded her. She blinked in uncertainty as to where she was, hoping that it was a nightmare.

Except for the pain in her head, she was completely numb to the rocky terrain she was lying on and certain every bone in her body was broken.

"Mom…Dad?" She listened for a response, trying to sift through the millions of sounds that echoed in her head and the barrage of nocturnal life that surrounded her on every side. "Mom?"

Suddenly, she began to sob and the eight legs that had materialized while she had been confined at the laboratory abruptly came alive. They ripped through her back and torso and she screamed out in terror and pain. Fine, hair-like threading began to stream from the mark upon her stomach, quickly wrapping around her and the eight appendages.

"Help me!" She cried as the webbing quickly covered the majority of her body, hooking on twigs and vegetation and snaking its way around everything within reach. Then suddenly, catching on a nearby broken-down tree branch, it shifted its course and completely covered the branch and then stopped.

Lana caught her breath and continued to cry as hours passed. She closed her eyes for what seemed a few brief moments; however, when she awoke, the sun was slowly cresting in the east. She could see Samuel wandering aimlessly through a distant patch of trees.

"Samuel!"

He glanced at her strangely then slowly hobbled in her direction.

Lana watched him as he gradually made his way toward her. He was still in his underwear; his body was scratched and bruised and a massive lump marred the side of his face. Without saying a word, he dropped to his knees beside her and hugged himself as he shivered.

Samuel, are you okay? Where's Mom and Dad?

He lowered his head and began to cry.

Lana questioned him again. "Samuel, where are Mom and Dad? I need them to help me get out of this thing."

Slowly, he raised his head and through reddened eyes, he stated…"They're gone."

Lana shook her head in disbelief. "No, Samuel. They can't be gone. They were going to take us home."

He pointed a shaking finger at the drop-off just beyond a cluster of pine trees. "They're down there…in the camper."

"No, Samuel. No! Mom and Dad are okay. They were going to take us home!"

Samuel hid his face behind his hands and readily wept. Lana wanted desperately to reach out to him, hold him in his time of need, and also, to just be comforted herself. Her heart was tearing in two; however, because her body was caught up in the strands of thread, all she could do was cry along with him.

Time passed slowly and Samuel dried his eyes. He attempted to loosen the threading encasing Lana, but the fine strands were too strong. They were clear, like fishing line, yet they were tough as fencing wire. So, gathering some of his clothing that had been scattered about the area from when the camper had crashed, he dressed. Then, he gathered Lana's clothes and covered her. And, regardless of her objections, Samuel left and went in search of help.

Lana watched her brother as he had climbed up the hill and disappeared out of sight. That had been over a week ago and she hadn't seen him since.

Lana had somehow managed to calm herself, and the eight legs completely vanished within her skin. One would have a difficult time believing she had any abnormalities; for, the only sign of anything strange was the hourglass-shaped mark alongside her navel. It slightly resembled a tattoo, like the ones she had seen on some of the older teenage girls. Those girls may have thought it looked cool. Lana didn't.

Tarren

Lana walked slowly along the many shops and small businesses that made up the small town of Tarren. Tarren was quiet, except for the hustle and bustle of the people who scurried in and out of the few eateries that were open for lunch. The smell of broasted turkey filled the teenage girl's nostrils and her stomach began to growl. She had no money to buy food.

She could see Bear Mountain in the far off distance. She recognized it from the big patch of evergreens that resembled that of a bear standing on its hind legs— possibly fighting to protect its cubs. Tears filled Lana's eyes as she thought of her mother, father and Samuel. The last time she had seen them was when they had been trying to escape the military compound where she and her brother were being held. That was over a week ago.

Her stomach growled again, this time much louder. Fortunately, her father had taught her and Samuel some survival techniques and she had been able to eat a few berries in the woods she knew were edible. That had been more than a three days ago and she really needed something to eat.

Lana walked slowly in front of the shops as her

sandals scraped along the sidewalk. Fortunately, she had found her shoes amongst some of the wreckage from their camper; and, her mother's idea of keeping them hooked together to keep them from getting separated, certainly paid off.

She hadn't asked anyone for help when she had arrived in the small town, fearing they would take her back to the military compound. Besides, who would believe her story that she had eight hairy legs that grew from her back and webbing that streamed from her stomach? They would think she was crazy or on drugs. Also, she had no idea how to get in touch with her mother's sister, Aunt Christine, who had divorced and remarried a few years ago. Her name was changed. That was the only relative she knew who existed.

Lana's mind drifted from her aunt to the wonderful scents of blueberry muffins and apple turnovers. She watched as one of the shop keepers, who was busy baking muffins and pies, was setting the fresh baked goods to cool on a stand near the front door of his shop in the attempt to attract customers. The aroma was tantalizing and Lana's stomach rumbled unmercifully. She just needed something to hold her over until she could get home; then, she'd stuff herself until she felt she would explode. Briefly pausing, she wondered what she would do then. She shook her head, and decided she'd worry about that later. Right now, she felt like she was starving. She wandered in the shop's direction.

A plate bursting with orange and banana muffins sat on a fancy wooden cart just outside the bakery. She gazed at the warm pies with their flaky crusts and fresh fruit, and muffins the size of softballs. Her mouth drooled and the temptation to just grab one and run was overwhelming. She knew she could never do such a thing. However, as she stood there ogling over the baked goods, a piece of one of the muffins, which had expanded from the heat, suddenly split in two. Half of a warm banana muffin tumbled onto the cart. It was like heaven had just granted her wish.

Knowing the piece would have to be thrown away, she quickly glanced around, grabbed the piece and stuffed it into her mouth. The muffin was warm and delicious; and, she wished the single bite could last forever. She quickly chewed and the piece was gone.

The shop keeper, returning with another tray of baked goods, noticed her putting food into her mouth. Placing the tray on a nearby table, he hurried from within the shop.

"You, girl! Stop!" He pointed a shaking finger in her direction.

Lana spun in shock to see the baker rushing toward

her. She turned to run.

"Stop!"

Lana was terrified. Her heart pounded within her chest as she pushed her way through several by-standers who had stopped to stare. Someone in the crowd attempted to grab her arm, but, somehow she had gotten her sandal caught on something and she tripped.

Lana stumbled from the crowd of people and landed face-first in the street. Tears rushed to her eyes as loose gravel from the road scraped along her face, hands and knees.

"Owww!" She began to cry.

Suddenly, the eight legs that had disappeared for more than a week tore through her skin and top.

Chapter 6

Evan sat on a bench beneath a small shade tree eating a piece of shoofly pie. He had walked from his home located just outside of Billet, a small town just over a mile away. He figured he'd walk a hundred miles for shoofly pie if he had to. It was his favorite and he couldn't understand why. He could never remember his mother serving it; but, then again, he couldn't remember much of her anyway. The last time he had seen her or his father was over one-hundred years ago when his father had chased him from their home in Rockworth, approximately forty miles west. He had been seven then.

Evan had been a fun-loving child and had always loved baseball. His father would take him to local games where men from the surrounding towns would face off for the county championship. The winning team would get their picture posted all over town and each player would receive a large, succulent ham from the local butcher. Game day was always Evan's favorite day and he looked forward to baseball season for months —the popcorn and soda, wearing a baseball cap, and cheering the teams on. However, while he was at one of the games that was being played just beyond the base of Bear Mountain, he had been bitten by something that had crawled from beneath the bleachers. Thinking it was a regular bug bite, his father rubbed some salve on it and they continued to watch the game.

By the time the game was over and they had left for home, Evan was feeling quite ill. And, by bed-time that night, he was extremely sick with a rising fever. The local doctor was summoned, but a severe thunderstorm was brewing that evening and the doctor was unable to arrive until the following morning. Evan violently shook with severe chills as sweat poured from his body and joints and his muscles ached with excruciating pain.

"Mommy, am I going to die?" He had quietly asked his mother who sat beside his bed.

Sadness filled his mother's eyes as she held his small hand and bravely answered. *"No, honey, you won't die for a long time; maybe not for a hundred years."* A small smile crested her lips, then quickly disappeared as she gently brushed a lock of dark hair from his damp forehead. She remained at his side praying to God to heal her child and for the doctor to arrive quickly. Eventually, she fell asleep in a chair with her head lying on her son's small chest.

Hours of fitful sleep went by as Evan tossed and turned; and, sweat soaked his pajamas and bed. Pain like he had never felt before brought him to full alert and he wanted to scream, to cry, do anything to rid himself of it; but seeing his mother finally resting, he remained quiet and suffered in silence. Tears poured from his dark eyes and he gripped the sheets with fisted hands. And, when the transformation began, he couldn't control it. Eight hairy legs tore from the skin on his back and webbing rapidly streamed from his stomach. It quickly wrapped around both him and his mother till his mother's head and upper torso where completely encased. Evan's mother struggled in an attempt to break free and breathe. She was quickly dying. Evan cried out for help.

Evan's father immediately rushed from his bedroom to Evan's room and was horrified to find his wife being suffocated, not by his son, but by a hideous mutation.

"*Mary?*" he shouted. "*What's happening? Where's Evan?*"

Evan stared at his father through large, red, gleaming eyes, and his normally blonde hair was jet black, wild and stood straight on his head. Except for his small arms and upper torso, he had completely transformed into something that resembled some sort of hideous bug or spider. This wasn't the little boy Evan's father had taken to ball games and loved very much. This was a monster that at the moment, was killing his wife. Evan's father ran to the kitchen to grab a butcher knife.

Evan turned his attention toward the young teenage girl who was slowly moseying along in front of the shops that were located across the street from where he sat. He guessed her age to be about sixteen or seventeen, somewhat younger than what he looked. She seemed odd, distant, like she was lost or something.

Tarren was a small town and everyone knew one another. And, though he remained to himself and only associated with the man he worked for and the man's daughter, Miss Diana, he was certain this girl was not a local.

He watched as she mulled over the baked goods in front of the shop where he had just purchased his shoofly pie. She reminded him of a cat that had spotted a chipmunk sleeping and was ready to pounce.

Because of his exceptional eyesight which had come with his transformation, Evan could see a piece of a muffin split apart and tumble onto the wooden slats of the cart. He then saw the girl immediately grab the piece and stuff it into her mouth. Mr. Thomas, the shop keeper, unaware she was eating a *spoiled* piece, hollered to her. Evan watched as the young girl hurriedly turned and ran.

"Dummy. Why didn't you just ask? He'd a just given it to ya', probably the whole thing." Evan shook his head. He knew this from past experience, from when he had first come to town many years ago and had been hungry.

Mr. Thomas, who was a young man then, would give him broken muffins, slightly burnt cookies, which were still delicious, and shoofly pie. All Evan had to do was ask.

Evan flinched as he watched the girl trip on the curb and hit the street. "Ow. That hadda' hurt." He shook his head again and took the last bite of his pie. Then, turning his attention back to the girl, he suddenly caught his breath. Eight legs were ripping through the back of her shirt.

"Hol-y shit." Evan rose to his feet.

*"**Someone** help me!"* Lana cried. The eight legs whipped about wildly as she stumbled on the road while attempting to get to her feet.

A few women nearby screamed while the men in the crowd consorted with one another on how to approach and catch the mutated teenage girl.

"Don't let her get away! She's probably dangerous!" one man shouted.

"Yeah, and imagine the money we can get for her! She's a freak!" another replied.

"No! I'm not a freak." Lana blubbered as strands of webbing poured from the hour-glass tattoo beside her navel and began to wrap around her torso and legs. She scrambled on all four into the center of the street and the men quickly followed. Suddenly, a black charger, refurbished to mint condition, turned the corner and slammed on its brakes. It was within feet from Lana and the crowd that had gathered. Music blared from within the vehicle and the driver, possibly twenty with chestnut-brown hair, dark sunglasses and a Yankee's cap, rolled down his window and shook his fist at the people.

"What the heck you people doin' in the middle of the road. I coulda' hit your dumb asses!"

"Oh, shut up!" one of the men in his mid-fifties, yelled. "Can't you see we have a million dollar prize we're tryin' ta' catch. Go home and polish your chrome. You're in our way."

The young man, named Trey Yanney, opened his door, stepped out of the vehicle and pushed his sunglasses up above his brows. He was tall, approximately six-foot and was clearly handsome. He stared at the people through silky blue eyes which matched his navy blue button-down shirt.

"Alright. Who's tellin' me ta' shut up? And, if there's a million dollar prize sitting in front of *my* car, then it's *mine*."

The passenger door of the vehicle opened and another young man wearing dark sunglasses climbed out. He looked to be about the same age as his companion; however he was slightly taller with striking features and blonde-hair. He wore camouflage pants, a t-shirt, vest and combat boots. His name was Ches Starling.

"Hey, Trey. Ya need a hand?" Ches asked.

"Nah. I think I got this. Just see what the old guy's talkin' about—what's in front of my car."

Trey glared at the people in the crowd. "Now—who was tellin' me to shut up and get outta' the way?

Ches walked around the front of the vehicle. His brows rose at what he saw. "Hey, Trey, ya' might wanna' take a look at what all these people are gawkin' at. It's a girl. She looks like somethin' outta' one of those horror movies. Come check it out."

"I don't have time for ugly chicks, Ches. Can't you see I'm about ready to kick someone's tail?"

The man who was in his fifties and had first shouted to Trey stepped within a hair's breath of him. His nostrils flared and the bands of his neck tightened. "I don't think you're gonna be kickin' anyone's tail, Yankee." He shoved Trey.

Ches looked at his friend then shook his head. He spoke to no one in particular. "Oh no, that was the wrong thing for him to do. Nobody pushes Trey and lives to tell about it."

Suddenly, Lana let out a scream. Spence Rodgers, who was a local from Billet, had been on lunch break from working in the local sewers in Tarren. He was a large fellow, in his early twenties. His red hair was grease laden and he was covered in filth; he smelled terribly of a men's latrine. Two of his buddies and co-workers stood beside him while he held his booted foot to Lana's neck.

"Ya'll can fight all ya' want. I'm takin' this girl with me and collectin' the money for 'er."

"Yeah, that's right. That's...right," Marty Brow and Booger Sheats confirmed. They were two of Spence's buddies who were just as grimy. "We're takin' this wench with us." Marty Brow announced proudly. Booger just nodded his head in agreement.

Trey used the distraction to his advantage by landing a solid right punch to the older man's stomach who stumbled backward as he doubled over in pain. Mayhem broke out as the women nearby attempted to get out of the way and the several men, observing the scene, joined in the fight.

Ches looked at his friend who was firing off one punch after another and sending men dropping to the ground. "Hey, Trey, ya' need any help yet?"

"Nah. Just get rid of those punks and get the girl in my car." He landed a boot to the side of one man's face. "Oh, and try ta' hurry up will ya', before I scuff my new boots."

Ches chuckled to himself and turned back to the three thugs surrounding Lana. "You sure you boys wanna' do this?"

"Hell yeah!" Spence hollered. "You're gonna' get the ass whoopin' of your life!"

Chapter 7

Evan watched as the events unfolded before him—
the girl, her face shoved to the road, and, the skirmish that
had broken out over the so-called rights to possession of
the freak. He had to do something to help her, especially
since she had definitely come in contact with the same
toxic insect he had so long ago.

Evan quickly assessed the situation knowing he could
basically take any one of the people involved in the brawl.
However, the two guys called Ches and Trey might be a
problem; especially, if he had to take the two of them on
together in addition to the crowd. He might not be able to
get the girl out without revealing his own abnormalities.
He had always been extremely careful not to transform in
front of anyone else, and, he didn't want to start now.

That would mean no more fresh baked shoofly pie—
that would be rough. He decided that if he was going to
do this, he would have to be in and out quickly, more than
likely, while the sewer rats and crowd were keeping Ches
and Trey busy.

Throwing the wrapper from his eaten pie in a nearby
trash receptacle, Evan removed his long leather coat and
laid it on the bench. It was the only coat he owned, so

he didn't want it getting torn. Then he placed his duffle bag alongside the jacket and proceeded in the direction of where the ruckus was occurring.

Spence Rodgers still had his foot on the girl's neck as she gasped for air and tears streamed her scraped, bleeding cheeks.

"Booger! Get up and kick that pansy's ass!" Spence shouted to Booger Sheats who was lying face down on the ground.

"I'll git im', Spence!" Marty Brow yelled. He settled himself into a wrestling stance. "I'll put im' in a full nelson."

Evan suddenly slammed into Spence and sent him stumbling to the ground. He then grabbed the girl's hand. "Come on!"

"I can't!" she cried. "I can't move!"

"Shit!" Evan cursed. Despite the webbing which was quickly encasing Lana's torso and eight legs, he bent and hoisted her over his shoulder. He spun around ready to run when suddenly he was tackled from behind and sent sailing along with Lana over the Charger's hood. Spence then grabbed Evan and pinned him with a thick forearm to the car.

"I gotcha' now!" Spence spewed into Evan's face.

"Hey! My car!" Trey drop-kicked the man before him and whipped around. "Get off my car, you saps!" He shoved Spence to the side and grabbed Evan. "Why, you little ass wipe, I ought'a kill you!"

Evan rapidly drew his knees back and immediately kicked Trey in the chest with both his feet. Trey flew backward into a parked mail truck and landed upon his haunches. He shook his head in mild surprise, that someone had actually knocked him down. Then, he rose to his feet, but was suddenly surrounded by three men.

Seeing his friend in distress, Ches cracked Booger and Marty Brow's heads together then tossed them to the side. "Ah, Trey, you'll never learn. Never turn your back on your opponent during a brawl, especially for a *car*." Ches grabbed one of the men by the collar of his shirt and flung him to the sidewalk. He then quickly landed a punch to another man's nose. Trey took care of the third.

Evan immediately jumped from the car, tossed Lana over his shoulder, and ran for his things on the bench. Grabbing them, he slipped between two buildings and out of sight. The crowd immediately followed.

"He ran in there!" someone shouted.

"Ah, this bites," Evan grumbled as he shifted Lana's weight. "Hang on." He reached up to retract the ladder of a fire escape. It clanged noisily as he pulled it down and climbed on. Fortunately for him, Lana was very light and he hadn't put much in his pack for his trip into town that day. He would hate to have to leave anything behind.

He's goin' up the fire escape! He could hear Spence holler.

"If this means no more pie, I'm gonna' be pissed," Evan complained beneath his breath. He continued to climb toward the roof of the building.

Spence quickly ran to the ladder and began to climb. Trey, who was not far behind, grabbed him by the pant leg and threw him in the alley. "Get outta' my way."

"Trey, whatcha' thinkin'?" Ches asked as he grabbed a rung and ascended the ladder behind his friend.

"I'm thinkin' we'll catch this guy on the roof, take the girl, then teach him a lesson about respecting other people's property. Just keep the others back and I'll do the rest."

Evan disappeared over the edge of the roof. It was a flat roof covered in gray shingles with several needing desperately to be replaced. An old brick chimney stood in the middle and there was nothing beyond that but blue sky. Evan's options for escaping quickly became few or next to none. "Great." He looked back at Trey who was climbing up over the rim of the roof; then, he ran toward the far end of the building. Trey followed.

Evan looked down over the edge—they were a good five stories high. He decided it would be best to turn and take a stand. He shouted at Trey, "I'm warning you. Don't come any closer."

Trey laughed. "You're warnin' me? Don't be absurd. I can kick your butt and then some. So, put the girl down and let's get this party started."

Evan sighed then laid Lana down and placed his coat and pack next to her.

Trey made the first move. He charged in Evan's direction and executed a round of kicks and punches that Evan skillfully blocked. Trey was somewhat shocked at Evan's expertise at defending himself. No one had ever been able to counteract Trey's moves before, except of course, Ches. He would have to attempt another approach.

"Hey, Trey—you doin' okay up there?" Ches's voice rose from the ladder where he was holding people off.

"Yeah. I'm fine," Trey replied over his shoulder. He returned his attention to Evan. "I see you have some nice moves. Very impressive. But, I've also noticed that you haven't struck a single blow. Are you afraid of fighting me?"

"No," Evan replied. "So, just leave and let me go about my business."

"Oh, and your business is with the girl who has turned into a creature?"

"Yes." Evan then glanced at Lana who stared back at him in terror. This was the first time he had actually looked into her eyes. They were large dark pools of fear, yet they were controlling and captivating like a hypnotist's tool.

Suddenly, he was unable to tear his eyes away; in fact, he was unable to move. He knew he had to turn his attention back to the pressing situation at hand, but, something held his gaze—held him captive to this girl before him. His senses were muddled, like oil and water which refused to intermingle. This wasn't good.

"Well, I have business with the both of you," Trey suddenly yelled. "You for scratching my car, and her, for paying for it!" Trey sailed through the air and kicked Evan squarely in the chest with both feet. "That's for earlier!"

Evan flew backward and teetered on the very edge of the roof. He grasped at air in the attempt to balance himself. He began to fall.

Lana screamed as Trey rushed over to Evan and grabbed for his hand. "Hold on, man!" Evan's hand slipped through Trey's and Evan toppled over the side of the building.

"Holy shit!" Trey froze as his heart banged within his ears and he feared what he might see lying on the road below. He hadn't meant to kill anybody; he had just wanted to teach the guy a lesson.

Holding his breath, he peeked over the edge.

"Gah!"

Suddenly, a hideous spider-like creature appeared

within inches from his face. It had eight flaring crimson-colored eyes, while its body was black and hair-covered. Eight long legs, strong as steel bands, gripped the side of the stone wall. Trey jumped back as the creature ascended the side of the building and thrust itself up over the edge.

"*Holy shit!*" he screamed as the creature effortlessly knocked him to the ground. Immediately, it began to encase him in webbing, with rapid, robotic-like movements, such as those used on an assembly line.

"*Oh, my god!*" He kicked his legs and threw one punch after another in an effort to fight the thing off; but, its strength was beyond anything human. His entire body, from his mouth down, was quickly encased in threading that was impossible to penetrate. He could barely breathe.

"Trey, what the hell's goin' on up there?" Ches hollered. "I'll be right there, man."

The last thing Trey remembered seeing was the flaming eight red eyes that glared at him in a state of hunger and the open mouth, the abyss from hell, that produced a set of hideous fangs. The sound of his own muffled screams rang in his ears as he was then lifted high in the air and slammed to the roof's surface.

Chapter 8

"**Oh** my god! Put me down! Put me down!" Lana wiggled her way out from Evan's arms and plopped to the ground. Her eight legs and webbing had disappeared and her clothing was tattered.

"What's the matter?" Evan asked her. He was dressed in only a pair of badly ripped jeans and his coat.

"What do you mean, *What's the matter*? You were a creepy looking spider just a minute ago!" She flopped back in the grass and stared up at the sky. Dark clouds were steadily rolling along the horizon and the air smelled like rain. "I need to get home; and I can't think straight. I must be having a nightmare."

"Come on. It's gonna' rain soon and I hate the rain." He stood over top of her and looked directly down into her face. She had long black hair and milky white skin; and her brows were thick and dark along with her flowing lashes that surrounded her bright dark eyes. Her lips were full and red as cherry candy. She was lovely.

"You're back to normal now so I think you can walk."

Lana tried desperately not to look at the young male's bronzed chest and muscular form. She focused on his eyes. They gently flashed from various shades of copper to russet, then from liquid gold to chocolate brown; and, as he moved his head and the sun fixated itself upon his iris's, the kaleidoscopic colors shifted from burgundy to black. She watched them in amazement.

Evan caught her stare and their eyes locked. He tried to tear his gaze from hers but it was impossible. "Stop that." He dropped his pack on her head.

"Ow, you barbarian!" She threw the pack back at him.

"Well, you keep doin' that thing with your eyes and I don't like it. Now, come on, I told you I don't like the rain and it's going to start any time now."

Lana scrambled to her feet. "So, where are you taking me? And, how do I know you're not some kinda' pervert or something?"

Evan snorted, "Yeah, I look like a real pervert." Shouldering his pack, he started to walk away. "Are you coming or not? I think we have a lot to talk about and maybe I can help you get home."

Lana thought about it for a moment. He definitely didn't look like a pervert; on the contrary, he was exceptionally good-looking. She decided to follow him in the hopes he might give her something to eat and maybe help her.

The silence was deafening as they walked through one field after another, and then into the woods along a dirt path. Every-so-often, she would glance his way; peek between the long dark strands of her hair to see his face. His look was stern, unyielding, yet very attractive with his boyish features. She wondered what his name was and where he might be taking her. "Hey, whatever your name is, can we stop for a little? My feet hurt." She sat down on a log that lay alongside the path.

Evan turned around and sat next to her on the log. "My name is Evan. Evan LaBonte." He put his hand out to shake.

Lana took his hand and replied, "My name is Lana. Lana Patterson." She removed her sandal and scraped the dirt from it. Her feet were black and she was in desperate need of a bath. Evan looked at them and grimaced.

They awkwardly sat in silence, each attempting to concentrate on nothing in particular to fill, the discomforting void.

"Come on, it's not too much farther," Evan suddenly announced. "And then, you can get a bath." He got up to leave.

The sound of a warm bath was inviting. Lana rose to her feet then gently touched Evan on the arm. "Hey, did I ever thank you for saving me from those people?"

"No. I don't think you did." He kept walking. "If

anything, I think you were trying to get me killed."

Lana stopped in her tracks. "How do you figure that? I didn't do anything."

Evan smiled. *"Oh, yes you did.* When that guy was fighting me on the roof, you tried to hypnotize me or somethin' by that thing you do with your eyes. That definitely gave *him* the advantage. Do you do that to all the guys you encounter, or just to me?"

"Humph!" Lana stomped her foot and stuck her nose in the air. "I do not! I mean I did not! I don't even know what you're rambling on about this thing with my eyes. Turn and look at me now!"

"No."

He continued to walk away. The air had become heavy and the first drops of rain hit the leaves of the trees then slipped to the ground below. A moment passed and the skies opened and it began to pour. Evan cursed as he began to run toward home and Lana followed behind.

Breaking through a heavy sodden mass of vegetation, they arrived at a small clearing where two log cabins sat next to one another. An older girl, possibly eighteen or nineteen rushed from inside one of the two log cabins. She was dressed in a red leather mini skirt and six-inch red heels. She was built like a model, long and lean; though her breasts, which bounced around like basketballs, were large and visibly extra perky. It seemed to Lana as if she had planned the entire event, from the rain to her skimpy, wet attire.

"Oh, my gracious!" she stated in a deep southern drawl, "Ya'll are soakin' wet!" She quickly opened the umbrella she was carrying and held it over her and Evan's head while locking her arm in his. "Evan, my goodness, where have you bin? I've just bin worried sick about ya'll."

They hurried toward the second log cabin that sat next to the one the girl had exited from. She quickly opened the front door and she and Evan stepped inside. "It's rainin' cats and dogs out there. And, speakin' of cats and dogs," she irritably glanced back at Lana who still stood out on the stoop, "who's the stray you have followin' ya'?"

"Her name is Lana." He motioned with his hand between them. "Lana, Diana. Diana, Lana." Shaking the rain from his hair, he removed his wet coat and hung it by the door. Then, he gratefully accepted the towel the older girl had retrieved from the bathroom that was just inside the cabin entrance.

Diana began to dry herself beginning with her large breasts, to her flat stomach, then along her perfect legs. She did it slowly, lavishly, as if it were an act of sensuality. It appeared to be a rehearsed act of sexual desire. Lana averted her gaze and blushed in embarrassment.

Evan paid no attention to the older girl's sultry actions; instead he turned to Lana who was still standing outside on the stoop. He motioned her inside. "Come on in here so I can shut the door." Then he turned to Diana. "Diana, could you get my guest a towel please?"

Diana abruptly halted her performance and stared at Lana, like a cat eyeing its prey. She irritably dabbed at her wet hair, then spun on her heels and went into the bathroom. Retrieving the only other towel, she returned to where the other two stood and irately tossed the towel to Lana.

Lana quickly dried herself making sure she did it without any hint of sensuality at all like the other girl had. She then handed the towel to Evan who also took Diana's.

Then, she glanced around the cabin. It was dark and dingy, lit only by one light. The walls were log, solid and thick, weathered through time. There was a small living room, a walk-in kitchen, a bathroom and a bed in an adjoining room.

The living room had a couch that had seen too many years of use, an old oak coffee table that looked to be something from Lana's late Grandmother's house, and an end-table. The lamp that was barely lighting the small cabin was hideous. It had a yellowed shade and a wooden base carved into a fish. Lana suddenly missed being home.

"You can get a shower if you like. There's a wash clothe and soap in the bathroom cupboard, but I don't have any other towels." Evan shrugged his shoulders apologetically and handed Lana her wet towel back. "Oh, and I guess you don't have any dry clothes." He tapped his forehead as if it would help his thought process; then, he eyed her up and down. "Well, I could give you some of my clothes, but they might be a little big. You're very slen..."

Diana quickly interceded. "Oh no, Evan honey; that won't be necessary. I can git her a few things together. I'm sure I have a lil' somethin' I can give 'er." Diana devilishly glanced at Lana while a wicked grin appeared upon her large, red glossed lips.

"Thank you, Diana," Evan replied.

"Yes, thank you," Lana whispered. Her head was lowered and she felt terribly uncomfortable. Here she stood soaking wet and dirty, not only before an extremely cute boy, but also before Diana who didn't like her—in fact, openly despised her. She hadn't done anything to the older girl; and, if Diana was being protective because Evan was her boyfriend Lana hadn't tried to interfere with that. Breaking couples up or getting involved in other's relationships was something she avoided.

It wasn't as if Lana wasn't attractive; several times

she had been told that she was very pretty. It was just that she had seen her friends go through one miserable relationship after another; and, she had always tried desperately to steer clear of the deadly woes of dating and love. So, she had never had a boyfriend or even been kissed. Besides, Diana was gorgeous, drop-dead gorgeous, and she wore expensive clothes. And, even though she was wet, she smelled wonderful, like the mixture of scents you smell when you walk into the perfume section of a store.

The older girl had nothing to fear of Lana coming between her and Evan's relationship—*if* their being boyfriend and girlfriend was the reason Diana disliked Lana so much.

Lana's chest began to ache as she suddenly missed her family and desperately wanted to go home. She turned and went into the bathroom and quietly closed the door behind her while the other two stood and watched.

Chapter 9

The bathroom was dark, pitch black. Lana felt for the light switch and flipped it on. The area was small, with a commode, tub and vanity top where several items, like toothpaste, a toothbrush, a comb; and, various other items that boys or men would normally use, were scattered haphazardly about. There was a variegated-colored, braided rug on the tan, linoleum floor and a clear plastic shower curtain which was pushed back to meet the wall. The one picture that hung on the wall was of a mountain range surrounded by a thick, pine forest. Lana stared at it briefly then turned her attention back to getting cleaned up.

A rash of goose bumps ran along her skin as she suddenly realized how chilly she was. Hanging her towel on a nearby rack, she decided she would take a bath.

She turned the water to extra warm; and as it fought its way through the old copper pipes, it spit and sputtered while filling the tub. Waiting for it to reach half full, she retrieved the soap, shampoo and a washcloth from the cupboard beneath the vanity, then quickly slipped from her wet clothing and stepped into the warm water.

The feeling was wonderful, the best thing she had experienced in over a week. She quickly washed her hair; then, planning on relaxing a little, she slid her entire body beneath the water to her nose and ears. That's when she heard harsh whispering coming from the other side of the door.

"But, Evvaaannn," Diana whined, "she can't stay heerrree. I forbbbiidd it!"

If there was a reply from Evan, Lana didn't hear it. She began to feel unbearably lonely as the thought and realization of her parents lying dead at the bottom of the ravine suddenly washed upon her like a wave. "Where are you, Samuel?" she mumbled as she slipped her head beneath the water, trying to drown out the feelings that were causing her eyes to tear and her heart to ache. Unable to believe her parents were dead, she began to cry.

Reacting to her upsetting state, the eight legs that had briefly disappeared suddenly returned. The pain was intense and Lana pushed herself up out of the water and arched her back.

"Oh, God!" She attempted to hoist herself out of the water; however, the webbing began to steadily stream from the mark upon her stomach and wrap itself around her body. The eight legs, fighting their way to remain free of the strands of webbing, thrashed about wildly, causing water to slosh over the lip of the tub and saturated the floor.

Suddenly, her human legs were ripped out from beneath her and her head cracked the porcelain. "Ugh!" She cried out in agony as she was yanked back into the water.

Blood began to seep from a gash at the side of her temple and she was being pushed beneath the surface.

"Help me!" She struggled to breathe as her head was being completely submerged and the webbing began to cover her entire face.

"**But**, Evaaaannnn, I don't want her herrreeee."

Evan suddenly held his forefinger to his lips as a sign for Diana to remain quiet. She looked at him strangely and readily obeyed.

"Lana," Evan called through the bathroom door, "are you okay?" He could hear water splashing onto the floor. "What's goin' on in there? I hope you're not making a mess." He perked his acute sense of hearing, which had also come with his transforming, to listen closer. He could immediately hear the younger girl's struggled breaths.

"Oh shit!"

"What's wrong?"

Evan glanced at Miss Diana, knowing he had to take immediate action. However, he had always made it a point to try and conceal his transformations and didn't want the younger girl's being found out either. That was one of the reasons he had insisted on not fighting when he had been on the rooftop; though, sometimes in an emergency his transformation, in front of others, couldn't be helped. Of course, those few who had witnessed his change had either thought they were imagining it or Evan would knock them out, like in Trey's case, so they would think they had been dreaming or hallucinating.

He knew Lana had transformed; he could tell by the scent she gave off. It was strange; alluring, captivating. Also, he could hear her breathing. Besides the fact that he knew she was drowning, he could hear the change in her lungs and chest. The whole situation was bewildering. He would have to get to the bottom of it all, but not right now. Right now, he had to get Diana out of the cabin and Lana out of the bathroom.

"Nothing. There's nothing wrong. I just don't want her making a mess in there. Maybe you could go get the clothes. I'll tell her to get out soon."

"Ohhhh!" Diana stomped her foot. "I don't wanna' go!"

Evan's look was stern, one she hadn't seen before. She quickly spun on her heels and grabbed the umbrella. "I'll be right back."

Evan watched as she ran out the front door and disappeared into the rain. He then locked the door behind her and turned back to the dire situation at hand.

"Lana!" He jiggled the bathroom door handle. "Dammit, it's locked." He quickly took two steps back and shouldered the door. It creaked loudly upon its hinges, but didn't budge; so, he kicked the door with his foot and sent it crashing to the floor. His reaction was one of a shocked whisper. "Oh, my God."

The bathroom was a disaster. The walls, vanity and floor were splashed with water and the shampoo bottle, which had apparently exploded, had sent its contents flying everywhere. Lana lay face down in the tub while the eight spider legs were wild, waving erratically in the air. Her human body was wrapped tightly in a cocoon and her dark hair floated around her to the surface while blood was readily oozing into the water giving it an eerie reddish hue.

Evan quickly grabbed at the flailing legs, but was immediately struck and sent stumbling backward nearly tripping over the door. "Sonofa…" He realized he would have to do something immediately before the girl died— if she hadn't already.

Yanking the shower curtain from its hooks, he lunged at the legs. They fought desperately to remain free but with his extraordinary strength Evan was able to overpower them. He wrapped them in the heavy vinyl curtain, then secured them with the belt he removed from his pants.

The vinyl would eventually tear, so he worked swiftly to get Lana out of the water and rolled onto the floor on her back. She wasn't breathing; and the part of her face he could see had turned slightly blue. It reminded him of his mother.

Evan tore at the webbing covering her face. "Lana! Lana!" He was unaware he had been shouting the young girl's name. "Come on! Wake up!" The eight legs slowly began to retract within her skin and the webbing began to disappear; however, she still did not move. Evan began to panic. "Come on!" He shook her wet, limp body. All color had left her face and she was now the shade of milk.

Suddenly Diana pushed him to the side. He thought she had been locked out. "How long have you been there?" he asked. She didn't reply to his question, but instead mildly scolded him.

"For goodness sakes, Evan honey, ya'll need to cover that girl up. She's li'ble ta' catch her death of pneumonia." She grabbed Lana's towel and tossed it over her. "Now let me show ya'll how this is done." Diana dropped to her knees and softly placed her strawberry colored lips on Lana's. She gently blew air into the younger girl's mouth then pressed lightly upon her chest.

Evan watched in mild astonishment feeling slightly embarrassed by the strange sensation that was stirring within him. He immediately turned, drawing his attention to the water and mess that would have to be cleaned up.

Moments passed and Diana then leaned against him and whispered warmly into his ear, her body tightly against his side. "Evan, honey, she's awake now. Do ya'll wanna' give lil' ol' me a kiss for bringin' her back ta' life for ya'?" Her southern drawl was thick and saucy. Then she smiled and puckered her lips.

Lana coughed and water slipped over her lips. Evan welcomed the interruption, as Miss Diana was now running her tongue lavishly along her teeth. He spun to assist the young girl.

"Are you okay?"

Lana looked at him through large, frightened eyes. Tears were full within them and she blinked to fight them back while attempting to figure out what had just happened. The color slowly began to return to her face; and when the realization of what occurred finally struck, her cheeks ran pink with embarrassment. She quickly scrambled to wrap the towel around her shaking, wet body.

"Don't ya'll worry, sweetie," Diana stated, "we already saw ya'll lil' bunches and it ain't nothin' worth talkin' about." She stood to her feet, walked over the broken door and grabbed a paper bag sitting just outside the bathroom entrance. She tossed it at Lana. "Here's some clothes

I was givin' to them there Good Will folks. Ya'll don't have ta' thank me; Evan honey can do that later." Smoothing the front of her clothing, she walked toward the front door. "Well, I haveta' go over to my mama and daddy's house right now, but I'll be right back. And, ta' tell ya'll the truth, I hope Evan honey's alone when I return." She slid into her red heels that she had removed at the door.

Lana held the towel and bag of clothes tightly to herself as she clamored to her feet and stumbled over the broken door. Pushing past Diana, she ran from the bathroom and into the adjoining bedroom and slammed the door. The tears she had so desperately held back immediately poured from her eyes. Evan sighed and leaned against the damp wall. A glob of shampoo ran within inches of his head.

Diana's heels clicked loudly across the door as she returned to the bathroom. She slowly straddled Evan's lap. "Evan, please," her skirt slid to the top of her shapely thighs. "Can't she leave?" Her lips parted and were suddenly on his as she pressed firmly against him. The scent of vanilla cinnamon mingled with that of her damp clothing and her long soft curls of blonde lightly brushed his cheek.

"Diana," he gently pushed her away, "I haveta' get this mess cleaned up. And, how did you get in here anyway?" She rose to her feet giving Evan a direct view of red panty beneath her short skirt. Then, pulling a key from within a small pocket, she dangled it before his face. "I made a copy. And I'll be back later expectin' more of what I came for." Exiting the small cabin, she slipped into the car out front that had arrived to take her to her parent's house.

Evan wearily climbed to his feet and made it a point to change the lock on the front door. He then wiped the gloss from his lips and returned to the situation at hand.

Chapter 10

DIANA

Diana's great great grandparents had lived on and owned a large 150 acre horse farm which was nestled between two of the largest mountains in the country. Fortunately for her family, her great great grandfather had one day, while farming the land, discovered a swell of oil on his property; and with the right investments and intelligent decision making, he had supplied the family with a great multitude of wealth.

A prosperous business opportunity had then brought Diana's great grandparents to the small town of Billet. They moved there so her great grandfather could commute to his extravagant, over-sized office in the big city of Aune', just twenty five miles away. His wife volunteered her time and knowledge of pesticides and chemicals to a local government agency. Her name was Marianne—later to be known as Grandmother Hobbs.

Evan had overheard that within the small military base stationed just outside Aune' top-secret testing was being performed on a group of mutated spiders—black widow spiders—that had infested the banks of the river on the outskirts of the town.

Due to the dumping of toxic chemicals being used for the advancement of military weapons, the spiders had become aggressive and discolored, and had abandoned their nests and offspring to scatter throughout the vicinity. Rumors of an elderly gentleman, who had been bitten by one of the spiders, had circulated throughout the area. The man had claimed that webbing poured from his stomach, and his limbs had become black, hair-covered and elongated. The locals had thought the man was just crazy; however, when the military became involved, the man suddenly disappeared and was never heard from again. This was the case with anyone who made this claim.

When Evan had transformed and run from his house as a young boy, he had been scared and alone, unable to ask anyone for help in fear they would try to kill him like his father had. He hid in alleyways, under people's porches and even in sheds. Hunger had driven him to the point in which he would eat bugs and flies, anything that crawled or wandered into his path. He began to enjoy the taste, the sense of snapping limps and crunchy shells, the struggle the insect went through in trying to escape. In Evan's mind, he had become a monster, a freak of nature, the exact *thing* his father had claimed he was.

However one day, as he was sitting on a bench in town, salivating over a ladybug that was trapped between his two fingers, he paused and watched a little boy across the street. The small boy was with his father. They were laughing as the man lifted the boy high into the air and placed the child on his shoulders. Moments passed and a woman joined them. She tickled the little boy and gave the man a kiss. Loneliness hit Evan hard in the chest and tears rushed to his eyes. Releasing the ladybug, he ran the back of his dirty arm across his wet cheeks and decided he was going to try to find help. Hiding just outside the military facility, he hoped he would find someone he could talk to, maybe an adult who would look kindly upon him and try to help him.

Diana's great grandmother had been working diligently for the government studying the infested spiders.

One day, while walking to her car in the parking lot, she discovered Evan sleeping in the brush. Having a son of her own and feeling the deepest compassion for the small, dark-haired, dark-eyed boy, she decided to keep his secret and take him in as part of her family. However, knowing the severe actions that the military would take and how the last individual had been experimented on and treated, she kept Evan's transformation and whereabouts hidden—even from her family.

The Hobbs' property was large, with slightly more acreage than the farmland they had previously owned. Two small log cabins, that had been used to house slaves years ago, sat on the farthest eastern point of the Hobbs' property where squirrels and a few other woodland creatures roamed freely. Marianne allowed Evan to choose which one of the cabins he wanted to live in; and, after he made his choice, they got busy cleaning it.

One day, she brought him a gift. *"Evan, I got you something today,"* she practically sang, as she opened the front door of the cabin and stepped into the darkness. She adjusted her eyes to the dimness—two candles were the only lighting.

"What is it? What is it?" Evan had excitedly asked, as he darted from his bedroom where he had been straightening his bed.

Unable to control her excitement, Marianne pulled a Golden Retriever puppy out from behind her back. *"His name is Hershey,"* she smiled, as she placed the puppy in Evan's arms, *"and he's all yours."*

Marianne visited Evan regularly, sometimes on foot and other times by horseback. She brought him food, clothing and the basic supplies he would need. She taught him to desire the taste of real food, steak, hamburger and fish, to deter him from eating bugs and other insects. She even educated him, taught him to read and write, all the things he would need to know to survive in a changing world. All the while, she worked diligently to find a cure for Evan who was aging in years but not physically.

Thirty years passed and Marianne's own son had long since moved away and had a family of his own. She was a great grandmother now and had continued to age while Evan remained young. He looked as if he were only sixteen. Unfortunately though, before a cure was found, Marianne had grown old and passed away, leaving Evan all alone.

Or, so he thought.

After the Hobbs were gone, their grandson, Carl, Diana's father, moved his family into his deceased grandparent's home. Diana was fourteen at the time.

One day, while riding one of the horses, the young girl accidentally came upon the two cabins and Evan outside gathering kindling for heat. Thinking he was only seventeen or so by his young boyish appearance, she hid within the nearby woods and eagerly fell in love. Every day afterward, she visited the cabins and watched till Evan would appear.

Months went by and the young girl was unable to suppress her feelings any longer; and, knowing Evan was away one day, she snuck into his cabin.

MEETING MISS DIANA

Evan perked his heightened sense of hearing to the

sound of footsteps lightly treading upon his living room floor. There were no windows and only one door leading into the log cabin so he was unable to peek in and see who was inside. He'd have to change that someday, but basically he liked it dark and secluded; he figured it was from his being part black widow.

When Hershey was alive he had never worried about locking the door. However, since Hershey had been gone for over approximately 35 years now, he'd have to start. And, before Grandmother Hobbs passed away, she had warned him of the dangers of the military finding out about his transforming. Sure enough, as soon as she was gone, they had come snooping around; but Evan prepared by filling his cabin with branches and leaves, making it appear empty and animal infested. It was a pain to clean up later, but it worked. They hadn't been back since.

Evan quietly climbed up the chimney and sat Indian style on the small overhang just above the door. With his acute eyesight, he could see a horse tied in the woods about 300 yards away. He frowned. Dark clouds were leisurely drifting overhead and the air smelled like rain. He hoped getting rid of this intruder wouldn't take long.

The front door slowly cracked open and a female stepped out. Evan could tell it was the person who had been hiding in the woods the past couple of months by the strong scent of perfume and strawberry lip gloss flooding his nose. Her scent had lingered throughout the woods. The smell was now overbearing. He almost sneezed.

The girl wore a hooded cloak and riding boots. He predicted she was young by the smell of bubble gum she was chewing and the gloss she wore. He hoped she would find his abode dark, dank and revolting and move onto another adventure.

Evan quietly shifted his weight and lay on his stomach as he waited. Suddenly, the girl ripped the cloak from her person and spun around.

Pulling a water pistol from her belt, she blasted Evan in the face with water. "I gotcha!" she proclaimed proudly in a deep southern drawl.

Shaking off the surprise, Evan leapt from the roof, knocked her backward off the stoop and landed on top of her. The young girl continued to fire, hitting Evan in the eyes and nose.

"Give me that!" Water was bad enough; however, to have it squirted in his face, Evan was irate. He pried the red plastic gun from her fingers and tossed it.

"Hey! Give that back! I was only foolin' with ya."

Evan irritably swiped his arm across his dripping nose and chin. "I don't like water," he snapped. He hopped to his feet and stared angrily at her and was surprised to find that she was nearly the picture perfect likeness of a young Marianne Hobbs. The girl was beautiful with honey blonde hair and bright blue eyes. From her face and childish prank, Evan thought she might be fifteen; however, she was built like that of an eighteen year old with large, over-sized breasts and the body of a woman. Her skimpy attire didn't help. She had on a low cut plum-colored blouse that revealed entirely too much cleavage, a small pair of cut off jean shorts and a pair of long black riding boots. Evan thought she looked more like she was going to a bar than out on a leisurely ride.

"So, how do ya'll bathe?" Diana smiled, displaying beautiful, large white teeth.

"What?"

She stood to her feet. She was tall and slender. "I asked: How do ya'll bathe, if ya'll don't like water?"

Who was this girl; and what did she want? Evan thought to himself. He looked at her strangely then irritably replied, "Angrily." Turning to head inside, he spoke over his shoulder. "What are you doing here; and why were you in my house?"

Diana grabbed her cloak and ran to catch up to him. She put her arm in his. He spun around and yanked away from her. "What are you doing?"

"Awe, don't be mad at lil' ol' me. I just wanted ta' have some fun with ya'. Look, I'll do a cartwheel for ya'." She sprinted across the yard and did several, perfectly executed cartwheels in a row. Evan chuckled to himself.

The young girl *was* trying awfully hard to impress him and he hadn't had any company for years, especially *that* cute.

"All right, I might forgive you for sabotaging me with the water. But, I won't forgive you for sneaking in my house." He scowled to himself, knowing the water was the worst; however, he couldn't give her the impression that snooping around was okay. He reached the door. "Well…" he turned to see her hurrying to catch him. She reminded him more of a Palomino pony cantering across the grass. He hid a small laugh behind a fisted hand while feigning a cough. At least she was amusing to watch.

"Can I come in?" she asked slightly out of breath, her blue eyes sparkling with enthusiasm. The strong scent of perfume emanating off of her was heightened by her perspiring body. Evan sneezed.

"No," he stated irritably, while running the back of his arm along his nose.

"Awe, why not?"

He stared at her through dark, almost black eyes. Her visit had suddenly become an annoyance.

"Because, you were already in my house—*uninvited. And*, you smell."

Her bubbling smile disappeared. She lowered her head for a brief moment and Evan thought that maybe she was crying. Suddenly, as if a light bulb had been switched on in her head, she perked up as her big blue eyes danced with excitement and her broad smile displayed triumph.

"I know!" she burst out; her southern draw was thick and exuberant. "I'll ride home and git a bath and come right back!"

"No," Evan stated flatly.

"I'll be right back," she chimed out, unmindful of his objection. She had quickly sprinted down the few steps and was half way across the yard heading toward the woods and her horse.

Diana had returned that evening washed and unscented to revisit Evan. Grudgingly, he had allowed her to stay for a brief time, until dusk when she raced back home on her horse bubbling with excitement that she had spent the evening with a boy she was madly in love with. Each day, she brought with her more affection than the last. Evan had thought that the puppy-dog kisses were playful, nice; however, there was just something missing, something he couldn't explain or decipher; an emptiness inside him that just wasn't fulfilled.

This continued until Diana turned eighteen, and to Evan's appalled surprise, she decided to move into the cabin next to his. The only advantage to her living next door was she brought him home-cooked food nearly every day...and electricity.

Chapter 11

"**Lana**? Are you okay?" Evan tapped gently upon the door to his bedroom. He could hear through the thick wood the young girl quietly sobbing. "Can I come in?" He then quickly stammered, "Only if you're dressed."

"No." The muffled whisper came from behind the door.

Evan paced briefly, unsure how to handle the situation. He never had to deal with anything like this before, not in all his 100 years on this earth. After Grandmother Hobbs' death, and except for the occasional visits form Diana, he remained practically in solitude. The only outside contact he had with others was when he worked at construction for Diana's father's company in town. It was the perfect job for his agility and climbing ability; also, it bronzed his skin in the summer and made him feel virtually all human. He would also, on occasion, visit Tarren for supplies and his very favorite, shoofly pie.

Evan stopped pacing and stood looking at the door. The old oak wood was nicked and scratched, darkened through time. He had replaced the latch handle, which had fallen off long ago, with a slightly more conventional knob that the girl now had locked. He did this to keep

Diana out of his bedroom which she continuously barged into.

He could easily shoulder the door, break it from its hinges, like the bathroom door; however, that would make for another repair that would have to be done; and, it would probably frighten her. Or, he could wait patiently until the young girl composed herself and decided to come out. *Nah*, he thought to himself. She might, and probably was, uncontrollably transforming again and that wouldn't be good.

He knocked again; this time a little louder. "Lana?"

"Go away!" She desperately shrieked. Her bare body was again being consumed in webbing and the eight flailing legs were tearing at the blankets and sheets upon the bed.

Lana fought back the tears and the change her body was going through—the metamorphosis into a hideous creature. She forced her thoughts to turn to Samuel, knowing he too may be experiencing the same fate as she, but worse. And, though he was stronger willed than she, he would need her help. She pressed her pale, delicate arms to the torn mattress and grasped the sides tight within her balled fists. She attempted to focus on her brother; however, it was no use. An image of her parents entered her mind and she lost her concentration.

The webbing quickly covered her face and she could

hardly breathe. "Help me!" she cried into the heavy mesh of silken threads. It was barely a whisper.

Evan's head instantly perked up as the muffled cry screeched through his ears and he groaned at the thought of breaking in another door then repairing it. Then, taking a step back, he immediately kicked in the door, sending it crashing loudly to the floor.

His bedroom was a mess, just like the bathroom. The down quilt he had been given years ago by Grandmother Hobbs was tattered, the white feathers strewn about the room and still fluttering throughout the air. Items from his nightstand were knocked to the floor; and, the candle, he kept next to his bed out of habit, broken in half. He mildly groaned then quickly made his way to the bed where he easily tore the webbing from Lana's face so she could breathe. She blinked her teary eyes and coughed. It was gravelly, sounding almost painful.

"Are you okay?" he urgently asked. She shook her head slowly and averted her gaze—no control in her eyes now.

Evan worked carefully to remove the webbing down to her chest. He was extremely cautious not to touch or even look at the parts he had never seen before, except, of course, what Diana was so eager to display. His thoughts momentarily turned to the feisty blonde-haired girl— her willingness to reveal almost anything to him. The thoughts of her quickly disappeared.

Fortunately, the eight legs were tangled and restrained within the heavy strands. Evan retrieved a spare blanket from the large armoire that sat in the corner of his room and placed it over her and carefully tucked it around her.

Lana watched him through wide, weary eyes; her embarrassment at being seen naked, fully coloring her cheeks. His touch was gentle, caring, and she couldn't help but watch in amazement at the kindness he was showing her, especially after she had destroyed quite a few things in his house and made such a mess. He sat on the edge of the bed next to her, neither said anything. The silence was deafening while both searched their minds for something to say, the situation was awkward. Then, he spoke.

"Are you okay now?" He glanced her way. His eyes were full of warmth, worry at her condition. No one had ever treated her this way before, only her mother and father; and *especially*, not someone of the opposite sex. She had been plagued for years with the pranks of her brother and his friends and she had thought that boys were more a nuisance than anything else. However, this stranger, looking to be eighteen—nearly a man—was different.

She quietly nodded her head, keeping her eyes to the hand-stripped logs that comprised the bedroom wall nearest to the bed.

"Have the legs retracted?" His voice was kind, gentle.

"Yeah," she barely croaked. Her throat was raw and her heart still mildly ached.

"Do you need help getting the rest of the webbing off?" Truthfully, he hoped not. His cheeks slightly blushed.

"No," she immediately responded, turning bright red at the thought. "It'll be gone soon."

He nodded his head in understanding then stood. "Well," he slightly stammered, "then I'll let you get dressed." He glanced around the room at the mess, then slumped his shoulders. "I'll be in the bathroom cleaning up."

Lana felt remorse for the problems she had caused him. She quickly whispered an apology. "I'm sorry."

Evan paused as if looking for the correct response, then responded kindheartedly, "I knew things were going to change the minute I decided to intervene in the fight over you." He picked up the door with ease. Backing out, he pulled it toward himself and left the room. There were open gaps on each side of the door where it was propped against the framing. Lana knew he could peek at her while she dressed if he wanted to. But somehow, she felt he wouldn't.

By now, the strands of steel-like threading had disappeared. The bag containing the clothes Diana had given her was torn, and the clothes were strewn about the floor. Lana slowly pulled the blanket back and looked at the red and black hour-glass shaped marking next to her navel. The strands of heavy threading were gone and had disappeared inside her. She shuddered at the thought.

Gently, she ran two fingers over the mark, studying it in the low lighting of the one lamp which lit the room. It was smooth to the touch, not raised or rough. It seemed a part of her, like a freckle or birthmark. She hoped it wouldn't be permanent, as with the legs or any of the other changes her body was going through. She had been shocked when she had seen Evan transform. It caught her off guard, had even momentarily frightened her. But, what terrified her most was the fact that she *too* was changing into that exact same creature, a spider-like creature. There were so many questions she wanted to ask, answers she needed to know.

Lana tossed the blanket to the side and slid her feet to the floor. She rummaged through the few articles of clothing scattered about, selected what she thought might match, then dressed.

After she was dressed, she got busy cleaning up the hundreds of feathers spread about the room, picked the things up off the floor and tidied up the bed the best she could. She felt bad about the damage she had done—ruining the quilt and all. Somehow, she would have to make it up to him. She glanced around the dimly lit room. There was the armoire, where Evan had retrieved the blanket, the bed and nightstand, an old chest and a three-drawer oak dresser that sat against the wall at the opposite end of the bed. A single picture adorned the top of the dresser. It was encased in a silver frame that held the portrait of a woman who looked to be the age of her own mother. The woman reminded Lana of an older Diana. She slightly grimaced at the thought that there might be two of them—two blonde females who disliked her so intensely.

Lana glanced at herself in the small oval mirror above the dresser. Her image was a mere silhouetted outline, mostly a shadow from the low lighting. Traces of dark circles lay like blankets beneath her eyes, probably from lack of sleep or from all the crying she had been doing. She made a meager attempt at wiping them away but the effort was futile. Running her fingers through her damp hair, she sighed, then called to Evan through the open gap on the side of the door.

"Hello? Can you move the door please, so that I can get out?"

"Oh, sure," he called from the kitchen.

The wooden floor creaked with age while his footsteps echoed throughout the cabin. He walked from the kitchen to the bedroom and slid his hands through the gaps on each side of the heavy door and easily set it to the side.

An involuntary smile stretched along his face as he ran his gaze from Lana's hair to her bare feet. The clothing Diana had given her was surprisingly suitable. It was a red skirt, similar to the one the older girl had been wearing earlier that day, but slightly longer, with a white turtleneck. Evan sighed; glad it hadn't been something out-dated or too revealing. The white turtleneck meshed well with Lana's long dark hair and large dark eyes. In fact, it made the young girl look quite attractive.

Lana noticed his gaze and blushed. "Well, the clothes fit," she stammered.

"Yeah," Evan agreed.

Lana noticed that he too had changed clothes. He now had on a fresh pair of dark jeans, white socks and a white t-shirt. His hair was wet and slicked back, accentuating his dark eyes which were surrounded by full dark lashes. They were exquisite.

Silence ensued momentarily with neither knowing what to say. Suddenly, Evan turned and headed back toward the kitchen.

"Are you hungry?" he asked over his shoulder.

"Yes," she answered in a low tone, trying to hide the anticipation in her voice. Her stomach growled and she hurried to the couch and sat down. She tapped her bare foot on the cool wooden floor and twisted her index fingers around one another on her lap.

"Are you nervous or just hungry?" Evan glanced her way out of the corner of his eye. He took a large knife from a drawer and began slicing pieces of ham on a plate; ham Diana had brought him a few days ago. He carefully laid the slices on bread that were spread thin with mustard then added a piece of cheese. Grabbing a paper towel from a nearby roll, he carried the sandwich into Lana. She grabbed at the sandwich a little too quickly and blushed at her overzealousness.

Evan smiled warmly and stated the obvious, "You *are* hungry."

"I'm sorry." She lowered her head in embarrassment. Her finger twirling began again as she stared down at the sandwich, her mouth watering uncontrollably.

"Then, what are you waiting for? Go ahead and eat. There's plenty if you want more."

As if she had been waiting for the flag to drop on an eating contest, she dove in. The taste of the ham and cheese was delectable; and the mustard, which she normally didn't like, was invigorating. She quickly ingested the sandwich, then looked up through pleading eyes, silently begging for another.

Evan watched through a slightly amused look, glad she hadn't refused the sandwich for the taste of something other than human food, like something that crawled or flew. However, when she looked up her eyes caught his and their gaze locked.

Her eyes were warm and enticing, yet cold and demanding while her face was expressionless. He suddenly couldn't tear his gaze away—away from her face and the trance-like spell she was subjecting him to. An unexplained energy surged inside him that sent his head reeling and nearly pitched him forward.

Drawing with all his might, power from the creature that was inside him, he yanked himself backward and toppled to the floor. He became irate.

"What'd the hell you do that for?" He quickly scrambled to his feet and made a meager attempt at composing himself while trying not to look into her eyes.

Lana looked at him dumbfounded, frightened by his abrupt actions and by what she now knew was an abnormal, unintentional action on her part. She quickly apologized. "I'm sorry! I didn't mean to do anything!"

Knowing she would begin to transform because of the lack of control of her emotions, Evan immediately attempted to diffuse the situation.

"Now wait," he quickly went to her and knelt beside her. "I didn't mean to be so..." he searched his mind for the right word, "...abrupt. It just caught me off guard, that's all." He picked up her napkin that had dropped to the floor. "Don't worry about it. Here, I'll get you another sandwich and something to drink."

Lana fidgeted nervously with the hem of her skirt then quietly asked, "Why is this happening to me?"

Evan finished making the sandwich, picked up a glass of lemonade that he had poured, and returned to the living room. Handing her the food and drink, he sat at the far end of the couch. He waited until she had taken a bite of the sandwich then he answered. "I know why." The sound of his voice echoed in the quiet while the rain outside beat in a steady monotone upon the cabin's wooden roof. "You were bit by a black widow spider."

He pulled his shirt up to reveal the four pairs of red and white stripes on each side of his abdomen. "So, was I. Ones that were infected over 100 years ago with a lethal toxin used by the military. Though, I thought they had recovered them all. At least that's what Grandmother Hobbs…

"Wait." Lana immediately stopped chewing and placed her sandwich on the coffee table. She swallowed the few morsels in her mouth. "I don't understand. You mean when Samuel and I were bit, it was by a black widow spider?"

"Who's Samuel?" Evan interrupted.

"My younger brother."

"Well, where's he?"

Lana wrung her hands together and lowered her

head. "I don't know. I haven't seen him for over a week." Her voice was barely a whisper, choked, as she held back the feelings tearing inside her. "He's been gone since the accident, when my parents were killed." She became silent. Then, she lifted her head and looked at Evan; her eyes swam with emotion which poured upon her soft features.

Evan knew she had a certain effect on him, yet he continued to gaze into her eyes, stare into the heated depths of warmth and iciness that emanated from deep inside the walnut colored pupils. He was trapped in their spell; it was tantalizing, a tormenting mixture of power and supremacy. Now, instead of fighting it, he welcomed it; drowned within the energy that flowed from her eyes to his, causing him to feel weak, almost paralyzed.

Lana suddenly looked away, breaking the contact which had visibly ensnared this boy within an unknown stupor.

Evan quickly drew back and gasped for air. His breathing was labored and his heart raced in his chest. He collected himself and looked at her sternly, unsure of how to react to the feelings and situation she was putting him through.

Lana quickly took a bite of her sandwich, making it a point not to look in his direction. She felt guilty after becoming aware of what she was now doing. However, the captivating feelings she experienced while doing it were amazing, enthralling; and, something inside her ached to do it again. She had never felt anything like it before. It was like an electrical current that ran from her head to her feet. She felt ashamed.

"What is that?" He was finally able to speak. "What are you doing with your eyes? It's like some kind of power you have. And, why do you continue to use it on *me*?"

"I don't know," she whispered.

Evan stood. His entire body was stiff, almost ached. He irritably attempted to shake it off but without success. He walked awkwardly into the kitchen.

Chapter 12

It was late and the cabin was lit by only one small lantern that hung near the front door. Evan was on the couch, tossing and turning; irritated by the roughness of the well-worn piece of furniture which was now his make-shift bed. He wore only a pair of jeans and no shirt.

The couch's material was coarse and scratchy to his skin and prevented him from getting a good night's sleep, and kept his mind alert to shuffle through the many pages of the events that had occurred earlier that day: his eating shoofly pie, involving himself in a fight, bringing home a girl who was bitten, and struggling with the sensations brought about by her eyes. She slept in his bedroom for the night—one night—until he could figure out how to get her home. Her parents were gone, and she had only one aunt whose whereabouts were unknown. Then, there was a younger brother, Samuel, who had been bitten and was missing. There were so many things he needed to discuss with this girl, things they hadn't talked about; because, as soon as she had eaten, she had fallen asleep.

Evan decided he would work on discussing them in the morning; though maybe it already was morning. It was difficult to tell until the front door would be opened—*one* disadvantage of not having windows.

He rolled his feet to the floor, then ran a hand through his tousled hair. Standing, he went to the kitchen for a drink; then he slowly shuffled to the front door, unlocked it and peeked outside. It was still dark and the night air was chilly, invigorating, and the rain, which had lasted most of the night had finally stopped.

Evan breathed deep, enjoying the refreshing briskness that settled upon the earth after a good downpour, the tingling sensation that filled his nostrils and the coolness against his face. Except for the occasional drop of rain slipping from the cabin roof or off of the foliage of a nearby tree, the silence of the forest was soothing.

He glanced through narrowed eyes into the blackness, able to observe everything as if it were daylight. He searched the few windows of the adjacent cabin for any sign of life inside. It was dark except for the small light that Diana kept on above the kitchen sink. He looked west in the direction of the Hobbs' house, seeing if there were any sign of her. Nothing. She hadn't come home, which wasn't like her; especially since she was so adamant about Lana being there. He wondered if something was wrong, not that he missed her or wanted her around; it was just strange.

Evan shut the door and returned to the couch. He sat

in the quiet, listening to the faint sounds of the darkened world outside as it was getting ready for dawn.

His attention was suddenly averted from God's normally designed plan to the sound of his bedroom door creaking open. He watched in silence as Lana gingerly stepped into the front hallway. The faint glow of the oil lantern reflected off the over-sized white t-shirt he had lent her, while her long dark hair was mussed and tucked behind her ears. Seeing him awake and sitting upright on the couch, she slightly blushed then whispered, "I'm sorry, I couldn't sleep."

He remained silent.

"Couldn't you sleep either?" she asked him. Her soft voice echoed in the dim lighting.

"I was thinking about your brother," he answered. "Did you say his name was Samuel?"

"Yes, I did." She looked down at her hands which began to wring nervously. "I need to find him."

"I agree," Evan replied.

Lana looked up in surprise. "You do?"

"Of course. First off, he's your brother. And secondly, he's been bitten and probably needs help. I'll leave first thing in the morning and search the area where the accident occurred.

Her large coffee-colored eyes brimmed with gratitude. "Thank you. I don't know how I'll repay you." She spun around to go back into the bedroom. "It won't take me long to get dressed, but I don't have any hiking b—"

Evan interrupted her and quickly stood to his feet. "Now hold up. I didn't say I was taking you. I can cover more territory on my own." Truthfully, he could cover miles in a matter of minutes if he transformed and used his webbing, however, he wasn't sure yet if he would do that.

Lana quickly turned around; mild confusion riddled her petite features. "But, I need to go too. He's my brother."

"No. I'm not taking you. With your inability to control your transforming, you might come across a dead bird or something and start crying. Then, what would I do, out in the middle of nowhere, you all wrapped up in your cocoon and those legs of yours swatting at everything in sight? Every time you get emotional you become a mess and nearly kill yourself. No, I'm not taking you, and that's final."

Lana looked at him in disbelief as he stood just feet away in the shadows of the darkness. The lantern's flickering flame played upon his bare chest and face, making him appear angelic. His flawless features were stunning, with lightly bronzed skin that defined his chestnut-colored irises: they sparkled eloquently. The miniscule flecks of golden copper gems within them twinkled like tiny stars and willowy lashes, thick like feathered wreaths, surrounded each. Gently, they stroked one another with every blink of his beautiful eyes.

His small, but perfect full lips, which were pursed beneath the rigidness of his smooth cheek bones, revealed no sign of reconsideration. His stance was also firm, clearly displaying the sinewy muscles of his arms and upper torso. They were impeccable, sleek, descending downward to meet the smoothness of his abdomen which completed his perfected physique. Four pairs of red and white stripes accented his torso, adding uniqueness and solidarity. This was undoubtedly not the body of a young boy, but the body of a young male coming into manhood.

Lana blinked her eyes, shocked at her uncontrolled impulsion to stare. She had to think of her brother, not this near Adonis-like figure standing before her. He would have to see it her way; but she had never been good at arguing with anyone except her little brother. Maybe she could think of this boy, near man, *as* her little brother, argue with him till someone had to come and referee. The idea immediately vanished as she continued to observe him in the darkness, his handsome features, promptness at authority and his bare chest which she was unable to draw her eyes from. She felt embarrassed, yet exhilarated at the same time.

The mixture of feelings was strange, something

she had never experienced before. Could these feelings possibly be love? She had never known what love was, except for, of course, with her mother and father and her brother. However, this was different. This was an emotion that stirred within her, like a smoldering fire whose flames were gently flickering, causing her insides to swirl with warmth. She shook her head trying to break the ties to this unexplained emotion.

"What's the matter?" Evan's voice broke through the silence. "You keep staring at me."

Lana was flabbergasted and turned several shades of crimson. Her wondering eyes immediately redirected themselves in the direction of the door while her thoughts raced in search of something to say; something to explain her desperate, visibly apparent, actions. However, Lana's tongue was quicker, and her lips parted and hurriedly blurted the first thing that popped into her frantic mind.

"Where's your girlfriend? I'd figured she would've come back." There. She said something—something stupid, but something.

Evan looked at her strangely. "Are you referring to Diana?"

"Well, yeah, who else?" she replied slightly more snippy than intended.

Evan chuckled and gave her a crooked smile. "Oh, no. She's not my girlfriend."

"She's not?" she volunteered a little too quickly.

"No; she's not." He sat back down.

Lana wanted him to elaborate, explain the situation a little better. But, instead of pressing the issue and making herself appear nosy, or worse, interested in him, she let the issue drop. Right now, she had to concentrate on getting him to take her with him; but how? Her toes gripped the cool wooden floor while she thought for a moment; then she walked over to the couch and sat down.

Evan watched her, making sure not to make direct contact with her eyes.

"I'm not changing my mind about you going, so don't come over here trying to convince me otherwise." His tone was set. "Diana tries that all the time and it doesn't work."

"Are you trying to suggest that I'm like Diana?" Lana glanced at him strangely through the fallen pieces of long hair that shadowed her face. She shuffled nervously in her seat.

"Aren't all girls like her?" Evan looked down at the girl's bare toes, folding and unfolding, like tiny fingers. He watched them, slightly amused at how clean they now were.

Lana's face scrunched up as a mixture of thoughts entered her mind. "Well, I'm not. I would never act the way she does."

"And how is that?" He raised a brow and looked at her.

This boy had done it to her again—put her on the spot. She stumbled on her words, as her muddled process of thinking frantically searched for the right response. Her hands gripped at the edge of the couch while she tried to invade every inch and cranny of her brain for anything intelligent to say.

"Oh, just forget it," she finally whispered.

"Then, why are you sitting on my bed? Your bed is back there." He pointed a finger in the direction of his room.

"Because..." Lana suddenly became desperate. She turned to him to test her new powers, capture his gaze within hers. "...I want to go with you to look for my brother."

Evan tried desperately to turn his head, tear his eyes away from her scorching brown-black eyes which now seemed larger and more powerful than life. Maybe it was because he was tired and hadn't slept; and, his body and mind were weak. Or possibly, deep inside he wanted to experience all that this power had to offer. Briefly, he wondered if he could transform, break the invisible bonds that were pouring from her eyes into his. But, it was too late; and, she had him trapped within her magical spell. She moved slightly closer to him and began to speak ever so softly.

"Evan—please let me go with you." Her words became low and hushed, a gentle wisp of sweet breath. "*Please.*"

Evan could smell the scent of her body as Lana shifted and her long dark hair fell gently along her shoulders. It was clean, refreshing, and his senses welcomed it, craved her scent like no other. His inner senses burned with a want and yearning he had never felt before; a surging desire to transform and wrap this young female within his indestructible webbing and entrap her within his cocoon. The feeling was tantalizing and riveting, an enchantress's charm which nearly sent him bounding upon her.

With every ounce of energy, he fought to stay away, fought the urge to attack her, and tear her to shreds. Or, was it something else?

Evan's inner beast readily began to come alive and he stiffened against its coming.

Suddenly, she looked away; and said, "I have to go to the bathroom."

For Evan, it was like being released too quickly from a wild carnival ride. His inner self twisted and turned, like the roaring flames of a blazing fire suddenly being doused with water. His stomach knotted as his head spun and he nearly fell face-first on the floor. Barely catching himself, he watched in a hazy stupor, as Lana stood and made her way to the bathroom, turned on the light and shut the door. He sat in a state of unfeeling consciousness and tried desperately to figure out what had just happened; what would possess him to *want* to transform, draw this young female who he barely knew, into his webbing and *devour* her? Was *that* what he wanted to do?

A few moments passed and Lana emerged from the bathroom. Her outward appearance was the same; however, her temperament was different, more assertive, as if something had changed while she spent those few minutes away from him.

Lana shook her now brushed hair free of her shoulders and stared at him. Triumph blazed in her dark, black eyes. Her test had worked.

Evan was extremely irritated.

"Whaddaya' keep doing that for?"

"Doing what?" she replied innocently.

He stood to his feet and slightly wobbled. This made him even angrier. "Damn it! Don't be coy with me. I could have killed you!"

"No, you wouldn't."

Evan was stunned at her offhanded, nonchalant response, her overconfident attitude. His body was still in a state of shock and he didn't feel very much like being nice.

"How do you know? What the hell's goin' on with you?"

"Because..." She approached him and gently took his arm pulling him down next to her on the couch. She looked directly into his angered face. There was no sign of fear or confusion in her eyes, or even the mystical swell that drew him to her—to desire to swim in those velvety pools of brown, then devour her entire being. This time, he didn't look away. "...I didn't use *all* my power."

Suddenly, it dawned on him, awoke him to the situation he was dealing with, the emotions he couldn't control. He swiftly ran his eyes over her entire body, from the crown of her dark hair, along the over-sized white t-shirt, to her clenching toes. He knew exactly what she was referring to when she mentioned *her* powers. *She* was a *female* black widow.

The female had power over the male.

Chapter 13

Evan quietly shouldered his pack. His thoughts remained elsewhere while a thousand questions ran through his mind and he struggled with each and every one.

The situation had suddenly become dangerous, not only for Lana, but now for him. He had never experienced anything like her powers before. She could control him—make him weak which he didn't like and would have to do something about.

It was daylight now and the morning air was chilly, but also refreshing. Evan wore his favorite long black leather coat, which was ample for the temperature, jeans, t-shirt, and his work boots. He glanced at Lana as she sat on the stoop slipping on a pair of hiking boots he had dug out from beneath Diana's bed. Yes, the older girl would be very upset; not upset that *he* had taken them, but upset that he had lent them to Lana.

She was still wearing the red skirt and white turtleneck Diana had given her and also a navy blue vest he had scrounged from his closet. Red, white and blue—the young girl looked cute, patriotic, but cute. Evan would have chuckled to himself if he weren't still upset by what had occurred earlier that morning—cute or not.

"I promise I won't get upset and transform." She finished tying the laces and stood up.

"Yeah, right," he grumbled. He turned and walked toward the path that led into the woods.

"And, I promise I won't trick you anymore with my eyes. I think I can control it now."

"Is that what you call it—tricking me?"

She hurried to catch up to him then grabbed him by the arm and spun him around to look at her. Evan caught himself slightly stiffening as she looked directly into his eyes. This only added to his irritation. "What now?" he asked.

There was no magic now or deep-seeded power seeping from her eyes to his, no mystical spell that nearly drove him to insanity. There was just the softness of her gaze that swam with an abundance of kindness, trying to conceal the inner fear that danced behind the warmth of her coffee-colored irises. His heart couldn't help but soften, feel compassion toward her for the loss she had recently suffered. "Thank you," she softly spoke.

Evan turned and headed back toward the path.

PINKERTON'S STORE
BILLET

Diana irritably tossed some change from her pink handbag onto the counter of the small general store located in Billet. The skinny, acne-faced, male clerk nonchalantly took it and expertly dropped each coin into the open register. Closing the drawer he turned his attention to the front door of the store as the chimes rang out and two young men entered. It was Booger Sheats and Marty Brow.

The clerk rolled his eyes then quickly retrieved a brown bag and some manila paper from beneath the counter. Laying one of the two pillar candles that Diana had purchased on the paper, he rolled it tightly then stuck it into the bag. Proceeding to do the same with the other, he then handed the bag to her while nodding his head mechanically.

Diana snatched the bag from his narrow fingers and turned to escape the aura of homeliness that was dampening *her* aura of beauty. She hated coming into the small town, to be surrounded by the local folk who she felt were menial, slaves to their backward ways. However, when her mother had asked for someone to drive into the diminutive, lifeless community to retrieve two candles, Diana had volunteered in hopes of seeing Evan; and also, in hopes of escaping her mother who was throwing one of her usual temper tantrums.

Being accused of being forty-four years of age instead of her actual forty-three, her mother, who was overly concerned about her age, was sent into a tizzy. So now she and her father were left to pamper and de-frazzle the woman they both loved who was absolutely gorgeous and in tip-top shape, however was always in need of reassurance.

Diana sighed, then she flipped down her large pink sunglasses that matched her ensemble of white skirt, white sweater and pink high heels. She then stuck her nose in the air and marched in the direction of the door.

"Hey there, blondie." Marty Brow suddenly appeared before her, blocking her way to the door. "How 'bout a little date." He was tall and thin with dark, slicked back hair, either from being wet down or from the oil emanating from his scalp. His smell was revolting and Diana immediately wrinkled her nose and openly scowled at his presence.

"Back off, grease ball," she rebuked in a southern drawl. "Ya'lls stench is curling my cashmere."

Her driver was parked just outside the front of the store and she could see him observing her from where he sat in the driver's seat of the Bentley. He opened the car door and began to get out. She gestured with a hand for him to remain where he was.

Diana attempted to step past Marty and reach for the door.

"Hold on, you." He grabbed her wrist. "I think I'd like to curl more than just your cashmere."

Diane yanked her arm away. "Get ya'll filthy paws off me you ill-bred flea bag!"

Seeing that his buddy had entangled himself with a *live one*, Booger, who was somewhat shorter and stockier with sandy hair and crooked teeth, approached Diana from the rear.

The isles in the store ran narrow with canned goods and bakery items. They enclosed her on both sides. Diana was trapped; the only escape was through the front door which was being blocked by Marty Brow. Another male suddenly appeared from behind him and spoke through the screen.

"What's goin' on, Marty?" It was Spence Rodgers. He was much taller and more muscular than the other two. He looked to be twenty-two. His reddish-brown hair was spiked and his icy topaz-colored eyes gleamed of sinister deeds.

"I think I got us another play toy here, Spence." Marty announced proudly. "Since the other one got away with that fella' with the long leather coat."

Diana glanced through narrowed eyes at the two young men before her. *Could they be referring to Evan?*

He had a long leather coat and had brought Lana to the cabin. Was Lana the other play toy they were referring to? Nah, Diana thought, though she listened with more interest.

"I'm not interested in this broad," Spence snapped. "I want that dark-haired creature girl."

Booger piped up from behind Diana. She had forgotten he was there and it slightly startled her.

"Spence..." He portrayed a mild speech impediment by clicking his tongue at the end of each word. "Just... let... us... take... this... one... along. Marty... and... me... can... share... and... you... can... have... the... other... one..."

Spence opened the door and stepped inside. The tiny bells above the door rang, signaling for the clerk to be attentive. The tall, skinny, acne faced fellow was no where to be seen.

Spence maneuvered himself past his friend and stood before Diana. He stood tall, looking down at her through an icy stare that ran the length of her perfect body from blonde hair to pink high-heels. His gaze stopped briefly at her chest where her cashmere sweater ran low and tight, revealing an extensive amount of creamy white skin. A wicked grin crossed his face and he reached out and gently touched her shoulder, feeling the softness of her cashmere sweater between two fingers.

Diana's heart raced and her stomach became slightly nauseous with the smell of his cheap aftershave. She refused to take her eyes from his and a staring contest ensued. Her hand tightened on the bag containing the two pillar candles and she shifted her feet slightly.

Spence could sense the presence of someone behind him on the other side of the door; it was a large hulking shadow. It was Diana's driver.

"Nah," he remarked as he smiled wickedly and winked at Diana. "Not today. Now, let's let the lady pass and get on with our own business."

Diana angrily shoved past him and Marty and walked out the door that Marcus was holding open. Her footsteps cracked along the sidewalk as she marched irately to the car and opened the rear door herself. She threw the bag containing the candles across the black leather seat and slid in. Marcus was in the driver's seat already starting the car: The air sparked with anger.

"Marcus," she snapped; her southern accent twisting with rage. "Tell my mother to buy her own damn candles from now on. Now, take me home so I can bathe. Their stench is suffocating me."

Chapter 14

Marty looked at their leader; a mixture of hope and disappointment riddling his crooked features. Spence returned his gaze then glanced at Booger who was just staring down at his feet and rocking on his heels.

"All right, go," he commanded. "But, I want you two at my place by 6:00 o'clock sharp." He looked at his watch. "That'll give you six hours to find out where she lives and ta' maybe scope the place out a little. In the mean time, I'll do some more askin' around 'bout that looser in the long coat and find out where he took the girl. It can't be far; they were on foot."

Marty was already out the door, like an agitated dog loosened from his leash, while Booger was close behind. Spence smiled to himself as he heard the tires of the 1979 Chevy Camaro squeal. It was the sound of excitement, a race to anticipation and exhilarating thrill. They would be having fun very shortly, even if it wasn't with the creature girl and her rescuer.

Spence's adrenalin began to stream wildly within his veins like a snake slithering through the grass. He decided to grab a soda to momentarily quench his rising thirst. Walking to the soda machine that sat just feet to his right in the corner of the store, he opened the door and selected a cold one in the back on the shelf. He was beginning to feel alive and invigorated, so for a change of pace, he decided he'd pay for the drink. Pulling a crumpled up dollar bill from within his jeans pocket, he laid it on top of the machine, turned and left the store.

Diana stared out the car window, watching the remainder of the small town go by and the coming of the countryside as it approached on both sides. She was angry, angrier than she had been in years. *How dare they touch her?* What was even worse, she would have to toss the clothing she wore. The three men's stench had permeated into the fabric's luxurious fibers and she could still smell it. "Damn them!" she muttered beneath her breath.

Marcus perked his head in her direction as he glanced in the rear-view mirror. "Did you say something, Miss?"

"Yes, I did, Marcus," she snapped, her southern accent twisting with anger. "Don't ya'll ever take me into that town again; ya' hear? And, next time, don't ya'll dare interfere before I git to knock some teeth out."

She turned her attention back to the rolling hillsides and thick forests. It was quiet here and normally she would enjoy the ride home, especially after they had entered the estate gates and started toward the cabin.

Marcus always complained beneath his breath about a

dirty car, but she didn't care. He was paid amply whether he was driving, washing the car, or coming to her rescue.

The sun was shining brightly, peeking through the few clouds overhead; and though the car's temperature control was set, Diana was hot and agitated—agitated by the stench clinging to her expensive clothing and agitated by the situation she had been confronted with. She vowed the next time she'd do some damage; put some vermin out of their misery. Her father hadn't invested in all those private self-defense lessons for nothing.

Plus, she was anxious to get home and missed Evan terribly. The thought of that girl being there alone with him boiled the blood beneath her skin, escalated the anger seething within her which was caused by the detestable imbeciles who had disturbed her at the store.

"Lana," she breathed her name with a vengeance, "ya'll had better be gone when I git back." She irritably removed her shoes and rubbed her feet.

Then suddenly her attention was drawn to something stirring in the woods. She shouted to Marcus, "Stop the car!"

Before the automobile was able to come to a stop, she had opened her door and was racing through the tall grass toward the woods.

"Miss?" Marcus rolled down his window and hollered after her. But, he was waved on as the young heiress disappeared into the line of trees.

The forest floor was jagged and rough, layered with any prickly thing Diana could think of. She screeched one absurdity after another as she gingerly stepped upon the foliage covered floor while curling her feet against the pain.

"What was I thinking?" she grumbled to a squirrel that hurried out of her path as she limped along. "That had better of bin Evan." She hoped she hadn't been seeing things when she glimpsed a long black leather coat and a person in: Red, white and...blue?

"Hello, Evvvaaannnn?" she hollered into the heavy foliage. "Where are you?"

"Diana?" came a reply. It was his voice, sounding magical and comforting at the same time. She smiled. And, despite the pain in her feet, she eagerly pressed forward.

Suddenly, red, white and blue apparel appeared through a break in the trees, alongside the black of Evan's long coat. A low growl escaped Diana's chest as she soon realized it was Lana. "So ya'll are still here," the older girl seethed through her teeth. An icy stare raced toward Lana, sending a cold chill up and down the younger girl's spine.

"We're heading out for a few hours," Evan stated.

He then looked at Diana's feet and frowned. "Where are your shoes?"

Lana quickly lowered her gaze. She couldn't help but notice Diana's bare feet, scraped and painfully curling and uncurling. Her gaze immediately ran to the hiking boots she was wearing—Diana's boots.

"Oh crap," slipped from her lips. This wasn't going to be good. She hurriedly glanced back up at the older girl, trying to avert her gaze while holding her feet absolutely still in hopes of making them appear invisible.

It was too late.

Diana instantly saw Lana's expression and looked down to see what the younger girl had seen. That's when she noticed *her* boots.

A strange smirk appeared upon Diana's face. Her feet were killing her and she wouldn't be able to wear heels for a week. Looking up, she stared hatefully into Lana's wide eyes. And, making her best attempt at not limping, she steadily walked toward the younger girl, while holding her gaze with an icy stare.

Diana came within an inch of Lana and looked down at her. The older girl's height of five-foot eight was intimidating, frightening, as she towered over the younger girl's even five feet. Lana felt herself slightly tremble.

Evan was standing just feet away. Surely he wouldn't let Miss Diana pulverize her, not out here in the middle of nowhere? And, *he* was the one who had given her the boots, assured her that it would be okay. She glanced in his direction and was shocked to see he wasn't there. *Where was he?* She looked back at the older girl and attempted to use her eye power. It didn't work.

Then Diana spoke; venom coated the words as she slowly enunciated each one. "Give me my boots, you little thief."

Without even thinking, Lana dropped to the forest floor and rapidly untied and removed the shoes. Then, she quickly stood and handed them to the older girl who still wasn't' satisfied.

"The socks too."

Lana obeyed.

Evan suddenly appeared from within the trees. "Quiet, you two!" He scowled at the sight of Lana's bare feet and Diana hurriedly putting her boots on. "We have company—undesirable company."

"Who is it?" Diana asked as she finished tying her boots and stood erect. "I wanna' know who's on my property."

"It's two thugs from in town. I think their names are Marty Brow and Booger Sheats."

The older girl's mind raced through the events that had occurred not less than an hour earlier. Her anger at the younger girl was temporarily forgotten and rage at the three who had approached her in the store sent boiling blood racing throughout her body. "How dare they follow me home!"

"They followed you?" Evan asked her.

"Yes," she spewed angrily. "After cornering me in Pinkerton's Store."

"What did they want?"

Diana looked at him. Antagonism flared in her single word. "Me."

Marty and Booger had followed just a few car's lengths behind the Bentley as it made its way through town and out toward the countryside. After the car had finally passed through the heavy iron gates at the Hobbs' estate, Marty pulled his dark purple Camaro to the shoulder of the road several yards back and parked. He waited until the taillights of the automobile disappeared as it made its way toward the house. Then, he opened his door and climbed out. Booger climbed out also.

He walked toward the gate and looked through the heavy bars at the enormous house that filled the horizon. "This must be Miss Highfalutin's place."

Booger just nodded. Then after a moment he asked, "How...we...gittin'...in, Marty?"

Marty ran his eyes along the stone wall. It disappeared on each side into a thick patch of blue spruce and soft needled firs. "We'll follow the stone wall; it has to end somewhere."

Booger nodded again.

The broad massive stone wall seemed to go on forever, deep into the heart of the forest. The foliage was thick and thorny, nearly impossible to break through in spots; and, in some cases they had to double back and circle around either a fallen tree or creek. Overhead, the canopy hung as a heavy layered quilt, blocking out the rays of the late afternoon sun, making it impossible to know the time of day. Marty reached in his pocket for his cell phone and checked the time. Three o'clock. They had three hours before they had to meet with Spence.

Booger had followed along quietly, keeping his thoughts to himself. Then he spoke. "Marty...ya'... think...we'll...find...our...way...back?"

Marty never answered; he wasn't familiar with the area and he had even debated on whether or not to turn around, forget about the blonde until another time. At least they now knew where she lived. Just as he was ready to turn around and head back toward the car, the sound of her southern drawl rang through the silence.

"Hello, Evvaaann? Where are you?"

Marty quickly crouched down, pulling Booger with him. "Ssshh!" He put a finger to his lips. About fifty feet in front of them, a flash of red, white, and blue crossed through the forest. Marty watched through narrowed slits as anticipation raced throughout his body. Suddenly, Lana stepped out into the clearing; Evan was beside her.

"Holy sh..." Marty breathed. He quickly pulled his phone from his pocket and hit the automatic dial to Spence's cell.

"Yeah?" Spence answered.

Excitement crawled along Marty's skin and hastened out in a harsh whisper from his rushing lips. Spence scowled as the hurried words collided with one another within his ear. "Slow down, Marty! I can't understand a thing you're sayin'."

Marty took a deep breath. "It's her!" he whispered more slowly this time.

"It's the girl you've been lookin' for..."

Evan quickly assessed the situation. Things were complicated now that Diana was with them. The younger girl knew of his beastly form and was also part black widow, so he could have transformed and gotten them out of there in no time. However, with the older girl present, this changed things.

"We need to move quickly," he whispered. He glanced down at Lana's bare feet then into her frightened eyes. "You'll have to ride on my back." He knelt down as she gingerly climbed on and wrapped her arms and legs tightly around him. He hooked his arms through her legs to hold her secure.

Lana rested her chin on his shoulder in the soft nape of his neck. Her breath was warm against his skin and wisps of balmy air reached his hair line and ear. She smelled of cherries; the shampoo she had used. It was nice, refreshing; and the scent of her skin was soothing yet invigorating. Evan's thoughts were becoming distracted. Angered at himself, he immediately shook his head, forcing himself to move.

"Hey!" Diana hissed. "Why's she gittin' ta' ride?"

Evan's revelry was broken and he looked at the older girl strangely, as if she had just appeared. Then he shrugged his shoulders and whispered. "You're the one with the shoes."

Diana shot an angry look at Lana who just cringed and looked away.

Evan started a slow jog in a southerly direction. He knew it was better to steer clear of the cabins, so he headed toward the large creek that ran through the center of the Hobbs' property. He increased his speed, hoping Diana could keep up. With her long legs, it shouldn't be much of a problem.

Lana immediately knew who they were dealing with; and though it had been Miss Diana that the two had followed, she knew who they would eventually target—

her and Evan. She shuddered at the memory of what had occurred less than a day ago. Her stomach roiled and she began to tremble.

Evan could feel her body shaking against him. "Lana," he asked as he scaled a downed tree and landed with a thud, "are you okay?"

"I'm scared," she whispered into his ear.

He tightened his grip on her and glanced over his shoulder trying to look into her face. His voice was gentle, reassuring. "I won't let anything happen to you."

Lana tightened her arms around his neck while smiling half-heartedly in an attempt to absorb some of the strength and confidence he possessed. However, she failed miserably.

The forest became dark, more ominous the farther into its center they traveled and Evan pushed his way through the dense underbrush trying to break through the heavy mass of foliage.

Monstrous sized trees, matured and possessing enormous amounts of leaves, waved grandly overhead. They swayed in the gentle breeze, displaying pride for their splendor and grace while an array of multi-colored deep-set green vegetation flittered upon their burly branches permitting only an occasional ray of the afternoon sun.

Lana suddenly stiffened.

"What is it?" Evan asked.

"I can hear dogs," she whispered.

"Yeah, I can hear 'em too; and smell 'em. Plus, someone else has joined them."

Fear echoed in Lana's voice. "I think it's the other one."

Evan didn't answer. He only picked up his pace.

They covered a massive amount of territory on the Hobbs' property where Diana often rode Sarge, her gelding. She briefly wondered if the horse ever got as tired as she felt now, with its lungs feeling heavy and its body overworked. She bent to take a breath. Evan and Lana were several yards ahead of her now.

"Evan," she attempted to keep her voice low, "ya'll need ta' slow down, I can't keep up."

"You have to try," he replied. He slowed his steps slightly.

"I can't." She halted mid-stride and dropped to her knees.

Evan stopped and gently placed Lana on the ground. His mind raced through the few options they had. He, then, quickly began to remove his shoes while the two girls watched in confusion. He handed them to Lana.

"Here, put these on. I know they'll be a little big, but it's better than being barefoot."

Lana shook her head. "No. I can't take your shoes.

What will you wear?"

"It'll be okay." His smile was warm and reassuring as he glanced into her terrified eyes. "I won't need them. Now, put them on and head toward the river. I'll meet you two there."

Diana was quickly at his side panting out a protest, "Ya'll can't leave us! Especially, *me* alone with *her*!" She pointed a disapproving finger at Lana.

"It'll be okay." He kindly placed her upraised arm at her side. "I'll meet you at the river; then we'll head back home." The sound of the dog and its owner were coming closer, though only heard by Lana and Evan. "Now, stay together and hurry!" He disappeared into the maze of trees.

Diana shot an irate look at Lana. Then she turned back in the direction of the river and snapped over her shoulder. "Come on."

Chapter 15

Evan broke through the underbrush from which they just came; then he doubled back in the direction of Marty, Booger, and Spence who had his dogs with him.

He knew he would have to take a stand and fight, transform into the powerful beast that could scale walls, run with magnificent speed, cover a large amount of territory quickly, and crush a human in a matter of seconds. His adrenaline flowed like hot lava, rushing through his veins to every extremity.

He ran through the forest with the agility of a lynx, oblivious to nature's carnage of its limbs and leaves, its oppressing entanglement of undergrowth. And, undressing on the run, he removed his coat from his body and tossed it to the side, then proceeded to do the same with his jeans and shirt. The sound of his breathing filled his ears and his skin thrummed with the ripping and tearing of flesh—the melding of man and beast.

Transformation came quickly. Each time it occurred, he had to catch his breath.

Evan was now one with the creature—slave to its barbaric nature and mindless to the behavior of man. Grasping a tree trunk within his eight elongated, hairy legs, he immediately scurried to the top, into its massive cover.

Spence pulled a small piece of pink fabric from within his vest pocket and rubbed it against his cheek. A malicious grin crested his lips as he recalled the scene from the day before when he, Marty and Booger had been breaking for lunch in Tarren.

Tarren consisted of a slightly higher class of people than what Spence preferred. So as a rule, he and the guys would stay confined in the small work shed on the outskirts of town where they punched the clock and ate their lunch. However, he had forgotten his lunch yesterday, so, fortunately for him, he went to the local deli for a sandwich. The owner had frowned in disgust as Spence ordered a ham and cheese, threw a few bills on the counter and left. That's when he spotted the young girl wandering around outside the bakery.

She looked timid and frail, almost lost, like someone he would enjoy coercing into doing vile and repulsive things against their will.

He had watched indifferently as she skidded onto the road and began to cry. He thought it was comical and laughed at her clumsiness. However, as her clothing was being ripped to shreds and her body transforming into what—a spider?—he forgot about his lunch and made a beeline in her direction. He was enthralled and captivated, drawn to her abnormality like a thirsting man toward water. The possibilities were limitless, and dollar signs flashed before his eyes like symbols on a slot machine spinning to a jackpot. He would have made her come with him if it hadn't been for the three who had interfered with his plan: Trey Yanney, Ches Starling and Evan LaBonte, whose name he had finally aquired from the not-so-cooperative bakery owner in Tarren, after "accidentally" knocking over a few of the man's displays.

Spence shook his head then smiled maliciously. It was time to pay the fiddler. He placed the small piece of fabric, a remnant of Lana's shirt, before the two large German Shepherds' noses. The dogs sniffed it cautiously; then perked their ears in the direction the girls had gone.

"Good boys." He patted them each behind the ears. Marty and Booger just watched; their faces glued in admiration.

"They got 'er scent," Spence announced. "They're headed toward the river. We'll split up—you two continue toward the river and I'll head southwest to cut them off."

The sun's silvery rays glistened off the many strands of Evan's webbing as he scurried atop one tree and swiftly sailed into another. A steady breeze stirred the many massive branches and shook the enormity of leaves.

Evan held tightly to the roughened bark of a limb—an exceptionally easy endeavor for his native beast. He twisted his head about listening innately for the three to approach.

The sound of foliage crunching beneath Marty and Booger's feet was thunderous as it rustled the tiny hairs upon his legs and raced upon his sensory nerves. Suddenly, he was aware that the third person, nor the dogs, wasn't with them. He would have to address these two quickly then locate the other.

Marty and Booger appeared through the heavy procession of trees.

"Damn," Marty complained. "Where they at?"

Booger replied, "I...don't...know."

"What *do* ya' know, Booger?" Marty snapped.

"I...don't...know," he clicked as he replied again.

Marty waved him away. "Well, I know one thing; I'd sure'd lik'ta get my hands on that blonde girl. She was hot!"

"Yeah...hot!" Booger agreed while nodding his head exuberantly.

Suddenly, Evan's webbing shot from the trees at lightning speed.

And, Booger screeched something indiscernible as the strands wrapped around his feet and slammed him to the ground.

"What is it?" Marty spun around to see the metallic strands rapidly encasing his friend. "What the shit is that?" He dropped to his knees and yanked on the threads. They were strong and durable, nearly tough as wire. "Damn!"

Booger's entire body was nearly covered. His terrified eyes bulged from his head as the webbing snaked nearer to his neck and throat and he anxiously pushed with his bound feet to try and get away. "Hhee...llp...me, M... aarr...ty!" His clicking increased with severity.

"Hold on, buddy!" Marty's hands shook as he pulled his switchblade from his sweatshirt pocket. Hitting the release button, he quickly turned and sliced through the strands that ran from within the tree. Then, before the threads could slip away, he reached up and grabbed them. "I'll teach you to mess with my friend—whatever you are!"

Evan's inner beast reacted immediately. He sprung from the tree and landed atop Marty sending him crashing to the ground.

Marty viciously swung his knife. "I'll slice you up, you monster!"

The newly sharpened blade raced along Evan's chest and blood sprayed from his incision. He drew back in pain and buckled to his knees.

A high pitched screech rushed from inside him and the beast responded with rage, becoming merciless and vengeful, driven by natural instinct. Fresh webbing streamed from its spinnerets as its powerful legs worked speedily to encase Marty in its cocoon—its hunger for revenge and blood nearly driving the beast to insanity.

Marty fought and cursed, but was quickly covered to his chest. He knew he was defeated and stared spitefully at the ominous creature above him. Saliva readily dripped from its bared fangs, melding with the beast's running blood. He felt it streaming along his face.

"Come on, monster! Go ahead and eat me!"

Evan angrily clamped down on Marty's shoulder, his razor-sharp teeth tearing deep into the bone. They bore into Marty's flesh, ripping every fiber and tendon, tissue and muscle, sending Marty into a fit of agonizing pain. He screamed out, calling to a god he had never acknowledged, and crying out for death to come quickly—take him from his miserable fate—the agony and horror he could not escape.

Poisonous venom coated each of Evan's jagged teeth as they plunged deep within Marty's skin. The venom pulsated throughout Marty's veins, fusing the poison and blood together while quickly racing throughout his body.

Slowly, Marty began to welcome it—welcome it as a refuge, a place of warmth and unconsciousness where the agony of deep set pain existed no more. His insides felt as if they were liquefying, turning to sap, and his mind readily became clouded to his surroundings.

Evan could no longer control the furious beast that raged within him. Blood leaked from the wound upon his chest, covering everything including his prey. He disregarded the screams and cries, welcoming them along with Marty's desperate struggle. This prey would soon be paralyzed or dead, succumbing to a liquid secretion.

Diana turned back to see Lana lagging behind. "Hurry up!" she hissed.

"I can't go any faster; these shoes are too big!"

"Well, ya'll are slower than an old nag!"

Lana could hear the panting breathes and the quickening footfalls of the dogs as they gained momentum and approached. *Evan, where are you?* Her heart pounded in her chest, not only with fear for herself and Diana, but also, for Evan. Something had happened, for the scent of blood was thick in the air, wafting into her nostrils like a flooding mixture of too many perfumes. Evan's scent was rich—a sweet aroma that aroused her senses like a flowery bouquet and called to her inner beast. The other was more acidic and bitter, foul to her senses. She knew Evan was badly injured.

She and Diana arrived at a clearing; just beyond was the river. The water raged with uninhibited power and authority, clashing with the boulders that lined its edges like infantry restricting its freedom. It doused the large stones with a fountain of wetness, gradually wearing away their hard exteriors, one drop at a time, a trillion drops per day.

Suddenly, one of Spence's two German Shepherds leapt out from behind a large thicket and landed in front of Diana. With bared teeth, it snarled, just daring her to move. She quickly turned and shouted to Lana, "Run!" Then, spinning on her heels, she took off in the opposite direction.

The younger girl spun to head in the opposite direction, but Evan's shoes, being several sizes too big, were cumbersome. She stumbled forward and her momentum sent her tumbling face first into the jagged sticks and debris on the forest floor.

"Ow!" Tears welled in her eyes and she gently touched the gash running from her temple to her cheek; it was the same area she had injured when she fell in the tub. Fresh blood ran warm upon her fingertips, collecting with it, dirt and leaves. The cut was deep.

Her vision was blurred and she felt nauseas. She slowly raised her head while attempting to remain conscious. Pain encased the right side of her face and she could barely focus.

The other dog raced from within the trees and both converged and sped toward Lana.

Diana hurried back to help her. "Leave her alone!" She picked up a large stick and swung it at them.

"Don't go gettin' all worked up in a sweat, little missy." Spence suddenly grabbed her from behind and pried the stick from her hand. "You're liable to dampen that cashmere of yours."

Diana burned with fury. "Ya'll get your filthy hands off me, ya' barn dirt!" She spun around executing the perfect round-house kick which landed a boot alongside his face.

Spence stumbled backward and caught himself mid-stride.

Angrily, he swiped a closed fist along his cheek where a welt had already begun to color. Then, he evaluated the situation a bit closer through narrowed eyes. A malicious grin crossed his face and his demeanor became sardonically pleasant. "A fighter, huh, I like that —makes things a bit more interesting." He began to circle Diana, study her like a hunter relishing in the fear emanating from its prey. He motioned her forward with a wave of his hand. "Come. Let's see what ya' got."

In all the years Diana was being tutored for self-defense she had never imagined her first encounter would be in the wooded area of her own property. She had always imagined it would be in the big city or possibly inside her home.

The sound of the nearby rushing river thundered in her ears and made it difficult to concentrate, center her focus on her opponent. Also, Spence was large, bulkier than any trainer she had ever come across. Hopefully, he would be slow and cumbersome and she could bring him down before he would do too much damage. She shifted her feet and prepared herself. Something told her this wouldn't be easy.

Spence lunged forward. He was faster than Diana had thought. She retaliated with a series of kicks and punches; but he was too quick. He grabbed her foot and yanked her forward. Her body slammed to the ground and Spence was immediately on top of her. "Gotcha!"

"Git off me!"

"No!" Spence spewed into her fuming face. He immediately swung a closed fist which landed alongside her temple rendering her unconscious.

Lana was helpless to the dogs' advances as they raced toward her. They covered the forest floor with ease, portraying the controlled strength in the movements of their muscular bodies. They jumped her from behind and quickly pinned her to the ground.

"Nooo!" she cried out. The two German Shepherds growled and snarled, daring her to move. Their eyes blazed with hunger, a desire for destruction. *"Please,"* she sobbed. "Don't do this!" She could feel her body changing, the metamorphosis from human to beast as webbing poured from her abdomen and the eight legs ripped through her shirt and vest.

Spence's attention was immediately drawn away from the blonde that lay before him to the younger raven-haired girl who was rapidly transforming.

"Nice," Spence sneered as satisfaction danced in his beady eyes. He shoved Diana to the side and reached the girl in a half dozen strides.

The beast in Evan was uncontrollable, a vampire thirsting for blood. His bared fangs dripped with venomous poison, aching to satisfy their need for sustenance and revenge. He had no mind for his victim—whether insect or human, while the taste of blood thick upon his pallet was waiting to become much needed nourishment and retribution. Evan's inner beast relished in the moment—a moment of satisfaction and fulfillment, though his own wound leaked, gradually drawing the life from his altered body. Suddenly, the sound of Lana's cries broke through his animalistic desire and he paused.

The cry was one of a female—a female black widow calling out in distress. His insatiable desire for a kill abruptly disappeared—his prey became insignificant, merely a possible snack for later.

Evan hurriedly bolted in the direction of Lana's voice. His eight legs carrying him swiftly across the forest foliage left a trail of blood behind him.

"**Back** off, you mangy mongrels!" Spence shouted at the two German Shepherds. He kicked them each with a boot. "This is *my* prize." He studied Lana's deformity, marveling at her inability to control the transformation from human to beast. The webbing was incredible—phenomenal—the legs stupendous, every paranormal lovers dream. They swatted at the air, waging war on anything that attempted to restrain their freedom.

"Geeze, that's sexy." Spence licked his lips. Then, he reached for one of the long, black appendages, but was quickly struck. "Damn it!" He immediately withdrew his hand. This would take some strategy. However, he didn't mind; the sight was beyond enthralling and exhilarating; and, if the urge to experiment with her hadn't been so powerful, he could have observed her all day.

He quickly ran his eyes around the open area, his thin near topaz-colored brows knitting together like two crooked fish hooks. He needed anything that would suffice for a make-shift net or rope.

The forest was filled with briar patches and scrub,

downed limbs of humongous maples that had been beaten by nature's fury and various breeds of fir trees that had cast their needles and cones which produced a layer of wild mushrooms and vegetation. Spence scowled. Then, his gaze fell upon the long grapevine growing wildly amongst several firs. Bingo—make-shift rope.

He yanked the heavy grapevine down from the tree; and, drawing a large hunting knife from the casing on his side, he cut it free. "This ought'a work," he spoke over his shoulder to Lana. He then headed back to where she lay.

Her legs were now wrapped within the webbing along with her entire body, face and head. She was completely still. Spence looked at her strangely then it suddenly dawned on him that she wasn't breathing. "Holy shit!" He quickly forgot about the grapevine and dropped to his knees. He attempted to tear at the strands; but, they were strong; it was like trying to break through wire. Realizing that she would be more fun alive than dead, he carefully, yet rapidly, cut through the strands with his knife.

The webbing quickly parted from her face, however, she still wasn't moving.

Spence sheathed his knife and placed his two fingers against the area just below her ear to feel for a pulse. Nothing. "Damn it all!" he shouted into her lifeless face.

He began to administer CPR, pound on her web covered chest with a fist. "Wake up! Wake up!"

I know, he surmised. *I'll get you down to the water.* Picking up her limp body, he hurried past Diana and toward the river. His feet scuffled along the rocky terrain of the clearing and he frantically looked over the edge of the fifty foot cliff for a place to reach the water's edge. He turned around and was suddenly slammed from behind. Lana flew from his grip and landed just inches from falling into the river below.

It was Evan; his inner beast raging with anger was responding to the female black widow's call. Though his breathing was labored and his blood dripped, splattering his enemy in crimson red, he bound upon Spence trapping him within his eight legs.

Spence was shocked by the creature's hideous, spider-like features, its large beastly head and hair-covered ominous body. He quickly realized what he was dealing with.

"Get off me!" He angrily fought back swinging one punch after another, yet his efforts were futile. He hurriedly assessed the situation, realizing that if this giant spider trapped him within its sticky webbing like that of a normal spider's, he would be done for. His ability to move would be quickly inhibited like the girl who had been trapped within her own powerful strands.

The only recourse would be the injury upon the

beast's thorax. Blood spilled readily from it: the wound was bad. This would be his way out. He quickly pulled his knife from his side, and calculating the spider's movements he rapidly drove his blade deep into the existing wound. Spence then rolled to where Lana lay and glanced at the water beneath them.

"Bye, bye, monster," he remarked snidely as he grabbed Lana and they dropped over the edge.

Chapter 16

Diana's eyelids wavered, resenting the idea of being opened while her head throbbed and it felt as if her skull was split like a cord of firewood. She had to force herself to focus, figure out where she was and what had happened. Groaning, she sat up, blinked her eyes and looked around.

It was nearly dark and the forest had grown ominous and murky, with shadows playing off the trees and overgrown brush, making them appear alive.

Diana shivered. The skirt and sweater she wore was filthy and her hands and knees were skinned. She rubbed her eyes with the backs of her hands then suddenly noticed Evan lying on his stomach just feet from where she was. He was partially hidden in the brush.

"Evan?"

She crawled to his side.

"Evan, honey? What happened to ya'll?" She gently touched his shoulder which was chilled to the touch. His face was pale and motionless and her hands shook as she rolled him over.

Blood covered his front and a nasty slice ran from sternum to kidney. "Evan?" Tears welled in her eyes and her words choked past the lump in her throat. "Ya'll had better not be dead!" She searched the dark for Lana through tear drenched eyes. They were alone.

"Evan...honey?" She glanced at the deep cut marring his front. "Please...can ya'll wake up? Please." Her fingers trembled as she touched his cheek, then moved to his neck. The area was lifeless, still. "Evan, ya'll hav'ta wake up." Tears ran freely along her cheeks as she wearily sat beside him on the ground. Carefully, she placed his head in her lap then she gently stroked his cheek.

She sat in the oppressing gloom, her mind attempting to sift through the events that had led to this. "Don't ya'll worry, honey, I'll stay here with ya."

The evening air was chilled, filled with threats of rain. She glanced up at the sky through tear-soaked eyes and scowled.

"I think it's about ta rain. I know how ya'll hate the rain." She pulled her legs tighter to her body then positioned herself so her hair and chest was covering his face. She studied his tranquil expression, the quietness and self-assuredness of his handsome features and tousled hair. Closing her swollen eyes, she listened to the sound of the rushing river and the nocturnal creatures as they chattered with life. The pain in her head was now just a dull, throbbing ache and she fought desperately to stay awake while envisioning the events that had taken the person from her that she loved the most. Hours passed and weariness enveloped her, making it impossible to remain conscious. Nodding off, she fell into a fitful haze of restless sleep.

Lana hurriedly drew a panicky breath as the rushing water sucked her beneath the surface and yanked her toward the river's jagged bottom. The pain in her lungs was excruciating, an implosion of the inner tissue and muscle. She was certain they were tearing with each mouthful of water she swallowed as she struggled against the strands of webbing that restricted her every movement.

Thoughts flashed before her mind, like fuzzy late night television shows made before her time. She thought of Evan and how he had transformed into the irrepressible beast, the beast that she herself was turning into. It was horrifying, a course in life she certainly didn't want to take. But, she felt she might have been able to manage if he was by her side, guiding her through the metamorphosis and the many changes her life was taking. However, after what she had seen, the possibility of him surviving was little or next to none. Just like the possibility of her not drowning—little or next to none.

Samuel's twinkling eyes and boyish smile flashed

before her eyes. She wanted to cry or scream; but most of all, she wanted to tear the strands of webbing from her body that inhibited her from swimming to the surface and race to find him. Now, he would surely be alone.

Her mouth opened as she hiccupped a sob and more water rushed to her lungs. She closed her eyes. Death would take her soon.

Suddenly, a pair of brusque hands grabbed her shoulders and heaved her to the surface. It was Spence. He immediately flung her to the ground.

Lana gasped at the intake of air as it cut into her chest and scratched at the saturated tissue of her lungs. The feeling of ripping and tearing in her body was agonizing and the gash along the side of her face was streaming blood. She coughed and gagged as water spilled over her lips and she thought she would pass out. Strands of wet hair laced with blood hung haphazardly over her face. She ached to push them away, away so she could breathe freely and stay conscious. Moments passed as she attempted to focus and get her thoughts in order. She shook her paining head sending the strands of long hair dividing and landing recklessly along her shoulders.

Spence was sitting on the pebbled shore. His head was bent as he laboriously drew in one choking breath after another. After a few moments, he swiped his wet arm across his face and mouth. He was soaked from head to toe and his grease-laden hair lay pasted against his head. He turned to Lana and stared at her. His leering ice blue eyes were hard and cold; their maniacal infatuation slid to his rigid jaw and pressed lips. Lana quickly looked away. Tears dampened her eyes as she thought of what he had done to Evan, and what he might do to her.

Spence then lumbered to his feet and looked around. His throat was scratchy as he spoke. "We're about eight miles east of where we went into the water. I bet your boyfriend didn't expect that move." He smirked. "Not too shabby, if I may say so myself." He coughed and made a brief attempt at shaking the water from his jacket.

Then, he suddenly turned to Lana; anger pressed his wet rust-colored eyebrows together. He bent to stare into her frightened, damp eyes while jabbing a finger to her hurt cheek. "All I have to say is: Marty and Booger had better not be hurt by that freak."

She winced with each jab; and the tears she had been holding at bay, poured from her eyes. The blood flowed freely, running along her wet neck and onto the webbing still surrounding her body.

"What? Does that hurt, little spider-girl? That's nothin' compared to the pain you're gonna feel after I get through with ya'. Then, I'm gonna' sell ya' to the highest bidder on the internet—auction you off." His laugh was sinister, heinous, and though Lana was warm and dry within her refuge of strands, she was trembling uncontrollably.

Her fear was intoxicating, like the bouquet of wine wafting before an alcoholic's reach. He grabbed her by the hair and yanked her head back.

His breath was in her face, intermingling with her own as she gasped in pain. A long, thick tongue readily slid from between his thin lips and ran from Lana's chin to her injured cheek. There, he paused briefly, swirling the large muscle within the blood like a straw stirring in a glass. Then, his tongue quickly disappeared into his mouth. He smacked his lips in show while an impish grin broadened his square jaw as he relished in the taste.

Lana's head began to spin and she thought she would vomit.

"Your blood tastes good, spider-girl. I can't wait to see how the rest of you tastes." His topaz eyes danced wildly.

"*Please*," Lana moaned. "Let me go."

Spence laughed aloud as he released her hair. "Yeah, right. You're better'n any wench I've ever had or ever will have; and, you're worth more than..." He paused. "Shit. You're worth more than *God*."

Chapter 17

Large over-sized droplets of rain fell from the dreary sky, infrequently plunking Diana on the head. She was dreaming it was her mother annoyingly poking her and questioning her about the candles. This was among the most pleasant of her gloom-filled dreams, most being horrific nightmares. She slowly opened her eyes and shivered. Her body was stiff from hours of being in a sitting position and from the chill that had settled upon the land. The morning sun was late to invade the darkness of the deep forest and heavy gray storm clouds thundered overhead. They rumbled along the sky like massive freight trains converging on the sun. The ground was damp with morning dew, and the rain that was beginning to steadily flow, spattered upon the enormous patchwork of leaves.

Diana looked down at her empty lap. It suddenly dawned on her that Evan was gone. She shook her head, unsure if she was still dreaming. She recalled hearing the shuffling of the forest foliage and broken uneven footsteps in the fog of her nightmarish slumber.

"Evan?" she whispered as she narrowed her eyes and gazed into the dimness. "Are you alive?"

Evan had been fortunate. For, while he had lain with his head upon Diana's lap with his body injured beyond repair, the creature within him had forced its existence upon him. It had brought him fully alert, alert to the severe pain and agony he had suffered during the fight with Marty and then Spence. His only means for survival would be to transform, allow the beast to metamorphose, accumulate the blood and tissue needed to stay alive. He needed to feed immediately. The beast within him forced him forward, despite the excruciating tearing of limb and tissue—the severe wound upon his chest melding with the hard exoskeleton of the spider's body. He would be only partially wounded as an arachnid and fully healed after he fed.

He darted into the forest, his thirst more than just a need, it was now a necessity. Snagging a large possum within his webbing, he quickly fed.

Evan moved swiftly through the dark forest and the downpour of rain which, even as a beast, he despised. The heavy droplets ricocheted off his coarse exterior; however, they didn't slow him down. He screeched in rage, angered by the absence of the female black widow, his female. He moved with ease and agility as his ruby eyes scoured the land before him and darted along the terrain, vigilantly watching for any human life—friend or foe.

His vibrant strands of silver webbing gleamed brilliantly before the descending moon. They raced through the air, adhering to each branch and limb in their path while sticking securely. Like steel bands, they were capable of holding the massive weight of an elephant.

Evan advanced quickly and quietly, blending in with the darkness of the nighttime sky and the shadows of the enormous trees. As a black widow, he normally would have easily been able to track the blood of a female black widow, especially Lana's. Her scent was extraordinary, unlike a normal arachnid's smell. It was an arousing aroma, a florid bouquet, something his own blood yearned for. However, Lana's scent was difficult to track since she had been submerged in water and carried so far away; and now, it was raining.

Evan headed downriver attempting to follow the faint traces of her blood as it mingled with the water and lightly clung to nearby rocks and branches along the river's muddy banks.

An angered shriek rushed from deep within his chest as he increased his speed.

Spence ran a hand through his wet hair and grinned. He recalled the walk back to his vehicle in the dark, which was nearly effortless. His familiarity of the land, from previously hunting in the area illegally, had been the key. And, while he had trudged through the deep forest, his clothing soaking wet and his boots sloshing loudly with each step, it had been a riveting experience. He had used his headlamp from work which he always carried out of force of habit. It lit up the forest a good thirty feet in front of him; but beyond that, the forest was nearly pitch black.

Lana was slung over his shoulder and she had wept the entire way. Her fear and anxiety had seeped through the hard exterior of her cocoon driving his curiosity wild. Inquisitively, he had run two long fingers along the resilient threads of her web restraint. The hard strands had quivered beneath his touch and he couldn't wait to explore the rest of his new treasure. He covered the several miles to his truck in no time—for, years of tracking game in the mountains on his frequent hunting trips, put him in exceptional shape.

Dawn was quickly approaching and the rains had moved on by the time they had reached the truck. Spence's eyes were glazed and glinted like topaz crystals—an open window to a maniacal mind. He quickly unlocked the truck's passenger door, opened it, then hoisted Lana into the passenger seat. The anticipation drew sweat to his pores as he slammed the door and stared in through the window at her propped crookedly across the bucket seat. She didn't look his way. Spence rushed around the front of his truck, opened the door and eagerly climbed in the driver's side.

Lana gazed numbly at the dashboard of the truck through the wet hair that hung limply around her face. The truck was newer with red leather interior and an emblem of a ram's head on the steering wheel. Several shiny knobs and gadgets littered the console and a new disc player sat proudly in the center. Spence sat Lana upright then leaned over her. He paused briefly and looked into her red, swollen eyes, each masked with dark circles. His face was within inches from hers as he smiled impishly and ran a finger along her bloody cheek. "Wouldn't wanna' have you flyin' out if we were in an accident." He grabbed the seatbelt strap and quickly buckled her in.

He held his stomach as he laughed out loud. The sound was wicked, fiendish, an endowment accrued from years of causing others to suffer. As his laughing subsided, he buckled himself in and turned the key. The truck roared to life and then he spun out onto the road. They passed Marty's maroon Camaro that sat just a few yards ahead along the shoulder. Spence leaned on the center console and suddenly snarled into Lana's ear.

"Marty and Booger had better be all right. I'm comin' back later ta' make sure." He reached behind the seat and pulled out a rifle, then rested it on the rack behind them.

Lana flinched and began to tremble uncontrollably. Grinding her teeth, she tried to keep them from chattering while also trying to keep from crying.

The forest flew by quickly as they raced along the road toward Billet, and the rows of small shoebox homes just inside town were a mere mixture of gray and white blur. A few of the locals were outside busying themselves with their lawns or just enjoying the temperatures which were mild for this time of year and Lana wished she could be one of them.

The outskirts of Billet came and went quickly. Lana glanced over at the collage of gauges littering Spence's truck dash only to see that they were heading south. Then, as they slowed and turned onto an old dirt road, the digital display read southwest.

He raced along the dirt road that ran parallel to a row of old abandoned shacks, then disappeared between two large corn fields. Then, he swiftly brought the truck to a halt in front of a small blue and white mobile home that was partially hidden by several large bushes and overgrown weeds.

Two junked automobiles, rusted and corrosion eaten, sat just to the left of the mobile home, and a small dilapidated shed to the right. A riding mower resting on its side, half assembled, was propped in the shed's doorway; it looked as if someone had been working on it then suddenly decided to stop.

Lana remained in a frozen stupor, though briefly she pondered why there would be a need for such a big mower: The entire area, except for the weeds in front of the trailer, was covered with nothing but dirt.

Spence's fiendishly gleaming face suddenly peered through the window at her and she jumped. He quickly opened her door, unbuckled her and tossed her over his shoulder. Then, he made for the front door of the trailer. The two German Shepherds that had attacked Lana in the woods were there to greet him. Spence shoved them to the side with a knee.

"Get outta' the way!" He maneuvered his way inside, and with a hip, slammed the door behind him.

The stench of dog urine and strawberry incense saturated the smoky air of the trailer, nearly making it impossible to breathe. Stacks of male magazines leaning against a torn leather recliner showed promiscuous women in various poses, while various tools were tossed haphazardly next to them. A small television set sitting in the far corner was playing while the wheels on the stand dug deep into the shaggy wine-colored carpet that was stained through many years of use.

Spence turned to stare at a young female, possibly nineteen, who sat on a well-worn sofa in the middle of the living room. She sat with her legs crossed, nonchalantly blowing smoke rings from her over-sized ruby lips which were directed toward the trailer's ceiling and perched in a perfect 'O'. Dirty blonde hair hung limply upon her head. It was tipped with black and red coloring and looked as if it had just been washed. She wore a low cut leopard striped blouse that was knotted at the waste and a pair of black satin pants that hugged every inch and curve of her very narrow body.

"I let your damn dogs in," she spoke through a puff of smoke. Her voice was saucy, slightly southern and high pitched. "Damn things jumped up on the side of my old man's car when he dropped me off. I thought he was gonna' kill the bastards." She tapped her cigarette into a butt-filled ashtray and blew a bubble with the gum she was chewing.

"So, what's that ya' got swung over yer shoulder?" She jumped to her feet and being much shorter than Spence she stood on her tiptoes, kissed him hardily on the lips and then attempted to look over his shoulder.

Spence's face beamed maniacally; and, teasingly turning away from her, he kept his newfound treasure at bay. "Just hold yer horses, Colette. This one's special." He rubbed his hand along the thrumming strands of Lana's cocoon. "We have us a new play toy."

The girl reached out a thin hand and ran it along the cocoon. Her green eyes sparkled with wickedness as she felt the movement beneath her fingertips. "Holy honey," she breathed. She laid her cigarette in another nearby ashtray which was also full. Then, she turned back to investigate with both hands. "What is this?"

He haughtily replied, "It's a web cocoon and inside is a spider-girl." He immediately turned around to show the young female Lana's face and head. "She's part spider; and her legs are trapped within the threads. Now, get outta' the way. I wanna' put 'er on the couch."

Lana closed her eyes as her body hit the cushions and her head cracked against the furniture's arm. She groaned.

"Oops! He's sorry, sweetheart." Colette giggled as she released a rash of phlegm-infested coughs.

Ches watched as Spence's black Chevy truck sped past where he and Trey were parked in front of Pinkerton's store. They had stopped to pick up night crawlers for a fishing trip they had planned for later that day. He stood beside Trey's Charger with the passenger door open. "Hey, Trey," Ches called to his friend, as he was coming out the front door. He was carrying a can of worms and a bag of snacks for the trip. "Wasn't that the knucklehead involved in the squall the other day in town?"

Trey quickly glanced in the speeding vehicle's

direction and noticed Lana in the passenger's seat. "Holy shit! *It is* him. And, he has the girl with him!" He cleared the few steps in a matter of seconds, tossed the items through the back window of his car and jumped into the driver's seat. The motor immediately roared to life.

The black Charger fishtailed as it sped out onto the quiet street and headed in the direction the truck had gone.

"Where you suppose he's headed?" Ches asked loudly over the roar of the automobile's engine.

"I don't know," Trey replied. He tilted his cap back pushing the chestnut-colored ringlets away from his face. "But, I'm surely not lettin' that low-life have the girl. He's liable to do somethin' sinister to her—the creep."

Ches's brows knitted together; his tone was condescending. "I thought *you* wanted her ta' sell?"

Trey held the wheel as the car skidded around a bend. Then, heading onto an open stretch of road, he tromped the pedal to the floor. The truck was just cresting over the hill two knolls ahead and disappearing on the other side.

"Nah, I was just pissed about my car. Though…" he scratched his head, "what that chick's worth is…" He shook his head and mulled over the figures for a moment. "Shoo, she's worth a fortune." Trey suddenly snapped a look at his friend. "And, I don't care what anybody says—that guy who took her *was* a spider, a black widow spider."

Ches held his hands up in innocence. "Look, I told you I believe you. It would have taken someone awfully skilled to take you out. Plus, there was the webbing to prove it. And, how else would he and the chick have gotten off the roof? There was only one exit and I was at it."

Cresting a second knoll, Trey down-shifted and immediately stepped on the brakes. A heavy cloud of dust hovered off to the right, rolling over several run-down shacks that at one time may have been used for housing livestock. A road, barely considered a tractor path, snaked through the field and disappeared over the hill.

"It looks like he went that way." Ches thumbed in the direction of the lingering dust.

"Yeah," Trey remarked as he shifted into second gear and slowly turned the car onto the road. "Shit. I'll need a good wash after this."

Ches looked over at his friend, his sky-blue eyes sparking with mild amusement. "I think you're gonna' have other plans, besides washing your car." He suddenly got serious. "Somethin' tells me this guy and his buddies are wackoes, idiots who wouldn't be afraid to hurt someone innocent just for kicks. The kinda person whose ass needs ta be kicked." They rode for a moment in silence.

"Why don't you pull over here and we'll go the rest of the way on foot." Ches motioned toward the edge of the dirt road.

Trey nodded his head and pulled partially into the field.

Chapter 18

As Lana lay on the couch, Spence leaned over her and studied her closely, staring into her terrified face. Excitement churned as molten lava within his innards and he began to sweat. Licking his lips, he could taste the heated pleasure of sadistic gratification rushing to his head.

Spence rapidly reached for his knife. It was gone, left behind where he had fought the hideous creature in the forest. His two buddies might be there also: he would check on them later. However, right now, the urge to open the girl's cocoon was driving him insane. He needed to get inside, investigate, then devise a plan on performing something sadistic. It would be something beyond maddening like a crazed artist that has lost his perspective. He would douse his canvas in paint with one wild slash after another, while creating a grisly masterpiece with a stroke of his flaring brush. Spence's creation would be horrifying, a devastation to human and beast. He would have to maintain control, leave some minute remnant behind for gain of profit. Briefly, he became disheartened, melancholy at the thought of the least amount of restraint.

"Damn," he muttered beneath his breath. Then, he turned to the watchful

young female beside him. "Get me a knife—a big knife."

Colette's head nodded exuberantly as she quickly turned, went into the small kitchen and returned with a large serrated butcher knife.

"What ya' gonna' do, Spence?" Eagerness played upon her face like a child on Christmas morning.

"Well, first, I'm gonna' cut this webbing off. Then, I wanna' check out them there spider legs. So, get back and give me some space. Those things are wicked as shit!" He looked into Lana's wide petrified eyes and grinned wildly. "Are you ready for this, little spider-girl?"

"*Please*," Lana begged, "let me go."

"No way, girly girl," Colette jeered with a snapping of her gum. She then touched the blood upon Lana's cheek and placed a drop on her tongue. "Mmm, sweet."

Spence began to slowly cut away at the strands of thread that held Lana captive. Each slice of the blade was slow and premeditated, a deliberated chore that caused Spence's hand to quiver and his body to moisten with sweat.

Lana turned her head and squeezed her eyes closed. Tears fought at the back of her lids and she thought of her family, their sudden demise and her suddenly being alone. A picture of Evan then entered her mind. He had said he would protect her, and she believed him—believed that he would make things right, possibly even find a way to cure her.

Evan, what happened? she thought. *You were going to protect me, plus help me find Samuel; but, now* you're *gone...you're dead.* Tears sprang to her eyes and she was unable to control their coming. The threads of her webbing grew.

Spence threw his hands in the air. "What the hell? The more she bawls, the more that webbing shit grows! Sonofa..." He shoved Colette to the side and began to pace. "I know what I'll do." A few strides and he was back beside the couch where Lana lay. Balling his fist, he landed a sharp blow to the side of her head. Lana's head snapped to the side and her tears immediately subsided.

"That oughta' do it."

"Yeah," Colette cackled as she bent and coughed.

Evan raced along the water's edge, the instincts of the beast running rampant with uncontrollable rage, livid at the loss of Lana's scent. He suddenly slowed to a stop, shook his head and released an earsplitting screech which reverberated along the forest walls and along the rushing river. The bustling sounds of the chattering forest immediately came to a halt and he held his breath. And, then perking his many millions of antennae-like hairs to the mild breeze that brushed along his rigid skin, he listened closely.

There was no sign of the female: she was gone.

Releasing a series of despairing calls, Evan then turned and headed in the direction of home. His arrival was swift and inaudible; and, without delay, he immediately began the transformation back into human form.

Bending and taking a deep breath, he tried to adjust to the metamorphosis taking him back to his human state. His entire body ached miserably from the transformation, the tearing of the skin upon his being, to the blood and juices of the arachnid that ran through his veins. This was something he could never get used to, no matter how many years passed or how many times he converted to the black widow's form. He hated the beast, despised it beyond that of anything else; and yet, he feared it, feared that maybe one day he would be unable to return to himself, return to who he truly was.

Evan quietly stepped onto the wooden stoop and grabbed the spare pair of jeans that hung on a hook just outside the front door. After years of transforming and destroying his clothes, he made it a practice to keep something there that he could dress into, preferably shorts; they were cheaper. Slipping them on, he then carefully opened the cabin door and peeked inside. He had known Diana was there by the tiny shafts of illumination that were filtering through the few cracks on the southern side of the cabin. She was asleep on the living room couch and a light was on. A box of Kleenex sat on the end table and a mound of tissue was beside it.

He could see a large discolored bruise which appeared to be an imprint of a fist that marred the side of her lovely features. And, though she was sleeping, she seemed to be in pain. A low growl rose from inside him and his body trembled with rage. *How dare they hit her!* Hitting a female was unforgivable. And, if Lana was harmed in any way, they would all pay—possibly with their lives. Scum like that were deplorable, irrevocably despicable. And, though Evan had never intentionally killed anyone, it wouldn't take much for him to start now.

His clothing was folded neatly and lay on the coffee table along with his boots and his pack. He was grateful Diana had retrieved them—he would have regretted leaving his coat behind.

He stepped lightly upon the wooden floor, not wanting to awaken her. The boards creaked beneath his weight and he watched as she turned on her side and settled back to sleep. If she were to awaken, too much time would be wasted explaining how he had survived after receiving such a fatal wound; and, time was a luxury he didn't have. Lana was in danger.

Evan grabbed his boots and socks, headed into the bathroom, and closed the door behind him. He flinched at the shocking image he saw as he switched on the light and glanced in the mirror.

His eyes were flashing between black and red and his walnut-colored hair was wild and unruly. Blood caked his entire front and the slice along his chest was long and deep. It was puckered along the edges, like a dredged ditch that had been carelessly filled in with blackened soil that lay on each side. There was no time for doctoring the wound or showering away the filth that clung to his body. So, he grabbed a wash cloth, ran warm water over it and washed his face. Rinsing it, he then ran the cloth over his chest and arms to remove some of the blood; all the while, wincing in pain with each touch to his wound.

"Damn," he muttered beneath his breath. He tossed the bloody cloth to the trash and quietly left the bathroom. Grabbing a shirt and a pair of shorts from his bedroom, and his long leather coat, he headed outside. Then, he hung the shorts on the hook next to the door to replace the jeans he was now wearing which would probably end up shredded.

He knew Marty and Booger had escaped their webbing restraints. The creature's strands of threading would have only lasted approximately five hours, then they would have disintegrated or washed away in the rain. And, though Marty was bitten, he had only been injected with a minimal amount of venom which would cause him severe pain for hours or possibly days. Then, he would be back on his feet again, no doubt, assisting Spence with his devious plans.

Evan's destination was Billet. There, he would question anyone who might know the whereabouts of Spence and his two buddies. He covered the distance quickly. The sound of Lana's cries still rang in his ears and the strange feeling of loss was insurmountable. And, hitting a female, like he assumed Spence had done to Diana, was unforgivable.

"Damn it. I'll pulverize those miserable lowlifes." He clenched his fists. "And, if they touch Lana in any way, I'll kill em'." His grumblings echoed around him, playing off the firs and pines, saplings and maples. They plastered his features with anger and misery; and his normally golden, velvety soft eyes continued to alternate between shades of crimson and black. He quickened his pace.

Trey and Ches swiftly covered the distance from the car to the mobile home and hid in the corn field. They both squatted down and observed the trailer from a distance. Spence's two German Shepherds were tied to the front porch. They barked and snarled in a maddening frenzy, trying to break free of their restraints. The front door hurriedly banged open and Spence stepped out onto the porch. His eyes blazed with fury, pulling his yellowed brows together at a thin downward slope and his jaw was tight, stretched to meet the bands of his bulging vocal chords.

"What the hell you'se barkin' at? Can't you mutts see I'm busy in here?" He descended the steps quickly, unsnapped their chains and set them free. Then, he spun on his heels and headed back inside.

The two dogs raced toward the corn field in the direction of Trey and Ches.

"Uh, Trey—I think we have a problem," Ches glanced at his friend then turned his attention back to the bloodthirsty dogs only a few yards away. Hunger for a kill burned in their gold black eyes and they moved at lightening speed.

"Yep. I think you're right."

"Should we run?" Ches smiled crookedly and raised a blonde brow. He felt his side for his knife.

"Nah," Trey replied. "It'd only excite them more. We'll stay."

The German Sherpherds broke through the first row

of cornstalks and easily glided through the rest.

"Welp, here we go," Trey grinned. He stood and Ches followed.

"You enjoy this, don't you?" Ches pulled his blade from its sheath.

Trey cracked his knuckles and flexed his right hand a few times. "I'm always up for a good challenge."

The first dog reached them at a raging momentum and quickly pounced on Trey. Its teeth were bared in a snarl and saliva dripped from its gaping mouth as it snapped at his throat. Trey stumbled backward but rapidly planted his feet. Grabbing the dog by its front foot and collar, he quickly flung it to the ground. The dog immediately reacted and quickly lunged for his throat again.

"You stupid mutt. Back off!" Trey threw a fisted blow to the German Shepherd's snout. The contact sent its head snapping to the side and blood burst from the dog's nose and mouth. A few teeth, coated with blood flew to the ground. Releasing a screaming yelp, the dog landed in a heap before Trey's feet. It lay for a moment dazed and out of breath, then slowly rose to its wobbly legs and shook its head. Turning, the dog ran back through the cornfield toward the trailer.

Trey swiped the back of his arm across his brow, then turned his attention to his friend. A staring match ensued between Ches and the other dog.

The dog snarled and growled, baring its sharp teeth in a show of supremacy. Its feet were planted and its body was arched, ready to strike while the hairs on its back stood straight.

Ches stood completely immobile, his blade held firmly in hand. He dared not to flinch, knowing the slightest movement would surely set a series of negative actions into motion.

"Ya' think he wants my blood?" Ches remarked lowly.

"I don't know, Ches," Trey replied in a mooted whisper. He turned slowly, careful not to make any sudden moves. "Maybe she wants a date. That's a female ya' know and she seems ta' be your type—contrary."

"Ha ha, very funny." Ches grinned. "If I recall correctly, that's more *your* type. Remember *Matalin the beast*?"

"Geesh, how could I forget?" Trey rolled his eyes and for a brief moment ignored the threat the dog was presenting. He reached up beneath his baseball cap and scratched his head. The impulsive movement drew the German Shepherd's attention and she immediately spun and lunged at him.

Ches reacted swiftly, and executing the perfect roundhouse kick, he caught the dog broadside and sent her flying to the ground. Angered, she quickly leapt to her feet and charged again; this time in his direction.

"Determined little wench aren't we." Ches flipped his blade within his hand and cracked her in the skull with the butt end of the knife. She yelped in pain then dropped to the ground. Blood trickled from a cut above her left eye. "Nice plan, Mr. Yanney," he then remarked.

Trey was brushing away the dust from his clothing. "What plan, Mr. Starling?" he questioned sheepishly.

Ches briefly studied his friend. Trey's actions were difficult to read sometimes and he knew better than to question his motives whether intentional or unintentional. However, most times his friend's procedures were right on the mark and got the job done.

"So, do ya' think she's dead?" Trey then asked.

"Nah." Ches sheathed his military knife and looked at the dog lying on the ground. "But, she'll be cranky for days."

"Sounds just like one of your women." Trey chuckled.

"No. You mean *all* of yours," Ches retorted. He then turned in the direction of the trailer. "Well, now that that's over with, how about we tackle the main dog?"

In a few strides, they appeared at the edge of the cornfield. A female's squeaky soprano toned voice crackled from inside; the sound was high-pitched and nauseating.

Trey raised his chestnut colored brows and wrinkled his nose in disgust. "I know that can't be our girl. Her voice was softer, more gentle."

"Yeah, this one sounds like a hyena."

Trey laughed and took off toward the trailer; he ducked down behind it. Then, signaling to Ches, he disappeared around the back. Ches ran in the opposite direction toward the shed.

Chapter 19

Lana awoke from a hazy stupor and lowly moaned. She had been dreaming of Evan.

Pain flashed through the darkness behind her lids and ran throughout her entire body. Slowly she opened her eyes and was finally able to focus. Her chin was resting on her chest and she was staring down at her feet.

She was clothed only in her undergarments and shackled by her arms and legs to the wall, mounted like a target for a game of darts. Her eight spider legs were also bound, however, for the first time, hadn't retracted into her skin.

Succumbing to the chore of lifting her head, she looked around. The room was dark and only a small amount of light filtered through the heavy layers of fabric that covered the two windows. A small table sat in the far corner and there was a wooden chair in the center of the floor.

"Where am I?" she barely mumbled. The slightest movement sent pain to the side of her face. She winced.

The door suddenly opened and Colette stepped inside. She flipped the light switch on and Lana blinked at the sudden brightness. Colette looked over at her then called to Spence. "Spence, she's awake." She then sat in the chair and crossed her arms and legs. Then, running her jade-colored eyes the length of Lana's body, she snorted, "humph."

Spence's footsteps pounded upon the linoleum of the trailer floor as his boots made contact with each nearing step. Lana's heart banged within her chest and nausea rose to her throat. She swallowed at its coming. *"Please*, let me go," she pleaded to the blonde-haired female. She thought of what Spence had done to Evan, ruthlessly killed him. And, while she hadn't known him very long, the pain for his loss was great.

Spence entered the room, large knife in hand.

"You killed Evan!" Lana was surprised by her own outburst. She knew it was terror clouding her judgment, forcing the harsh words she was shouting into her captive's face. And yet, she felt it was something else; something that was tearing at her heart, like the pain she felt when she lost her parents—pain for the loss of someone she loved. Was it possible that in such a short amount of time she had fallen in love with Evan? Fallen in love with the boy who transformed into a beast—an arachnid? Yes, she said to herself, she had. And, now he was gone. Tears poured from her eyes and she shook her head.

"Why? Why are you doing this?"

Spence approached in a watery blur and stared into her face. His eyes were hostile, jagged edges of glacial ice.

"Because, *you* are beautiful." He touched one of the eight spider legs which quivered, beneath his fingertips. Then, his gaze quickly raced to the hour-glass shaped marking upon her abdomen. Strands of threading oozed from miniscule-sized holes, too small for the human eye, and snaked along Lana's body. Spence's brows met as he watched in fascination. Colette was sitting in the chair enthusiastically observing. "Colette, come check this out."

She quickly scooted to his side. Her beaming face twisted strangely as she blew a bubble and cracked her gum. "Why is it wrapping around her body? Shouldn't it shoot straight out like Spider Man's? Now, *that* would be really cool."

"More than likely, she's unable to control it," he answered. "Just like her legs—she can't control them either."

Lana's body trembled and she gritted her teeth to keep them from chattering. The thundering of her heart pounded in her ears and her legs twitched sporadically within their restraints.

Spence touched his forefinger to her chest and traced

a line between her breasts to her navel. The webbing, quickly reacting, wrapped around his finger and raced up his arm.

"Holy shit!" He hurriedly sliced through the webbing. "You tried ta' wrap me up! Damn you!" His open palm cracked the side of Lana's face and she groaned.

"You wanna' play games with me?" He spun his knife within his hand and suddenly rammed it into one of the eight spider legs.

Lana's head flew back as a cry escaped her shaking lips. "Oh, my god!" The excruciating pain caused her entire body to shudder and her breathing to come in spurts.

"So, that hurts huh. Good, let's try another." He shoved the thick blade into a second leg; this time severing it at the joint. Lana screamed.

"**What** the hell's goin' on in there?" Ches pulled his blade, and scaling two steps at a time, he darted up onto the front porch. Suddenly the door burst open and Spence was there with his shotgun aimed at Ches.

"Gotcha!" He glanced past Ches's shoulder looking for Trey. "So, where's your friend?"

Ches's azure-colored eyes met Spence's cold glare: a staring match ensued. "I don't know what you're talking about."

Spence shoved Ches with the barrel end of the shotgun. "I'm not as stupid as ya think. So, tell me where your friend is."

Ches caught his footing and glared at the maniacal fiend before him without answering. He clutched the handle of his knife tighter.

"Colette," Spence shouted, "we have us some company. Grab my other gun and check out back for his buddy."

"How'd ya' know we were here?" Ches asked.

"Somethin' got a hold of my dogs, and it surely wasn't a coon. I could hear em' bawlin'."

"Spence!" Colette shouted from the back of the trailer. Spence turned for a brief second.

Ches reacted immediately by kicking the gun from Spence's grip. "Didn't your mother ever teach you any manners?" He then punched Spence in the face. "Don't point guns at people: It's not polite."

"Hold it right there!" Colette appeared in the hallway; she had Trey at gunpoint. Spence quickly grabbed his gun that was lying on the floor and again shoved it in Ches's face. The cold end of the barrel dug into his cheek.

Ches looked at his friend and rolled his eyes, then he muttered through the corner of his mouth. "So, ya had to get yourself caught. That's not like you."

Trey shrugged his shoulders and scratched his head.

"It's all part of the plan." He threw a thumb in Colette's direction. "Even ol' skanky here."

"Shut up." Colette cracked him alongside his head with the butt end of the rifle, then motioned him into the small living room.

"Ow, that hurt, you ruffian!" Trey rubbed the welt rising beneath his waves of hair. "I don't like forceful women."

"Like I give a rat's ass what you like," Colette replied then added, "Oh, and Spence, Booger and Marty are here; they're coming in the back. Marty looks pretty bad."

Chapter 20

Sweat poured from Lana's skin and she trembled uncontrollably. Her long, dark hair was plastered to her ghostly white cheeks and she thought she would vomit. The pain that rushed through her body was insurmountable. She wished for death.

"Oh, please, somebody help me," she barely whispered the words through her paining lips. Colette had made certain they were swollen, in addition to every inch of her face. Spence had been more interested in her deformities: the eight spider legs and strange webbing which had discontinued its growth and now remained still, just a few threads wrapped around her legs. He had severed two of the legs at their joints and had broken one other. He was saving the rest for later.

Lana could hear strange voices coming from outside the dark room; a moment of hope brought her to semi-alert. She thought she recognized them; however, she couldn't recall from where.

"Help me." Her words were brief wisps of air disappearing into the darkness. She lowered her head and waited, gathering what little energy and ability she could muster from her exceptional hearing ability.

Two more voices filtered through the thin wooden door; one was burdened with a speech impediment and the other just moaned lowly as if the person were injured or sick. Then, Spence's voice bellowed from the outer room into her ears.

"**That** spider freak will pay! Colette, Booger..." Spence shoved his gun in Booger's hands and took Marty around the waist. He helped him to the couch, "...watch these two till I get back." He then grabbed some rope and hurriedly tied Ches's hands and feet, then Trey's. Then, he shoved them each to the ground and spoke while dragging each one into a back room of the trailer. "Don't take your eyes off 'em for a second. Not for one second! I'll be back very shortly. Somebody has to pay for what they did to Marty."

Spence's feet banged along the flooring as he headed to the farthest room of the trailer where Lana was being held. Lana's heart jumped as he burst into the room. In a few strides he was before her, staring into her swollen face. He yanked her head back by her hair. She groaned.

"Where the hell's that boyfriend of yours?" he spat into her face.

Lana's body trembled violently and her teeth began to chatter. She shook her head as tears streamed her paining cheeks. Drawing all the strength she could possibly find, she stared into his eyes and mumbled accusingly, "You killed him."

"Somethin' tells me he's still alive. And, there's hell to pay for Marty's condition. So, tell me where I can find him."

Lana's body shook and her clouded mind began to spin. "No," slowly slipped from her broken lips.

Spence's face twisted with rage and he slammed her head against the wall. A dull cracking sound rang through her ears and she gasped at the lightening bolt of pain that shot through her head. Blood streamed from her nose and the corner of her mouth. Lana's spider legs quivered no more; they now hung limply from their restraints then slowly disappeared within her skin. She knew she would die shortly.

Spence pulled his knife from his side and quickly and accurately sliced through the bonds holding her prisoner. He slung Lana's limp body over his shoulder and headed for the door. "Before your mind is nothing but mush, you're gonna' show me where to find him. He briefly stopped, retrieved a pistol from the hallway closet and shoved it in his pants. Then, he loaded his vest pockets with additional clips.

"Colette, I'm goin' huntin' and I'm takin' the girl with me. I'll be back later. And, Booger, don't let those two out of your sight for a second. I'll deal with them when I get back."

Ches glanced over at his friend's back. Trey was lying on the floor, between him and the door. The room was empty except for the two chairs that their captives sat upon and various camping items that poured from the open closet which was packed full of junk.

"So, this is your great plan, huh? So, tell me, when do we save the girl?"

"No...talking," Booger stuttered. He was sitting on one of the chairs, leaning back on two legs; his gun rested on his lap. Colette had briefly gone out of the room into the bathroom and Spence had just left.

"Well, right now, Mr. Starling." Trey suddenly rolled, pulled his legs up and with all his strength kicked the back legs of Booger's chair.

Booger flipped backwards and the gun discharged into the ceiling. "Ho...ly...ly shit!" he exclaimed as he slammed to the floor and his head cracked the linoleum.

Trey quickly removed a small blade from within his ball cap and hurriedly sawed at the ropes binding his hands. Ches was busy slicing through his restraints with a tiny pocketknife that he had concealed within his belt.

"What's goin' on?" Colette shouted as she ran down the hall. "Booger, you toad! What the hell you doin' on the floor?"

Trey kicked the gun from her hands as she appeared around the corner; then, he tackled her to the floor. "Ches, throw me some rope!"

"Get off me, you loser!" Colette screeched, as she wildly kicked and screamed.

"Shut up, you mattress maggot. Just the sound of your voice is nauseating." His exaggerated glance raced Ches's way. "Rope please, Mr. Starling."

Ches was gathering the pieces of rope they had cut from their own hands and feet. He looked over at Booger who lay on the floor; he was out cold. "Sure." He tossed the rope Trey's way. "I just thought I'd watch you tame that tiger. She's a real alley cat."

Trey rolled his eyes and his brows arched beneath his ball cap. "I'd rather be sucking muddy water from a bucket."

Ches chuckled. "I imagine you would. Now, can you shut that broad up and let's get goin'. That maniac has the girl and no tellin' how bad she's hurt."

Colette coughed then snickered, "You're too late. That girl's almost gone; and, if she lives through the night, Spence'll kill 'er by morning."

Trey's look was one of repulsion, his normally congenial character disappearing within the rage behind his usually playful eyes. "If that girl dies, wench, I'm coming back here to personally break your legs."

He suddenly elbowed her in the face. Blood burst from her nose and she began to curse.

Dust clouded the air as Spence punched the gas pedal to the floor and headed toward the main road leading into town. He glanced over at Lana who was lying limply against the passenger door of his truck. Her legs and threading had retracted and she showed no sign of life. Spence grabbed her shoulder and shook her. "Hey, wake up! You need to show me where I can find your boyfriend."

Lana didn't answer. She couldn't, even if she wanted to. It pained her to do anything, even open her eyes. A searing buzz reverberated in her head and her body felt oddly numb.

"Hey! I said, *wake up!*"

Suddenly, there was a loud crash as something hit the back of the pickup truck. "Shit!" Spence cursed, as the truck swerved and he fought to keep the vehicle under control.

Lana opened her eyes. Suddenly, Evan appeared through the cloud of dust. He was on the hood and in his beastly form. Lana gasped at his size for he was as big as a rhino and black as night.

Spence smirked, "*Ho-ly shit.*" A smile broadened his face. "*He's here.*"

The beast within Evan was enraged, infuriated at the harm that had been done to his female. Quickly covering the windshield with webbing, he threw all his weight at the glass. His eyes blazed with fury and an incessant screech tore from his throat.

Spence slammed on the brakes, hoping to pitch him from the vehicle; however, Evan held tight, grasping to the metal with his huge legs. Yanking the pistol from his jeans, Spence then jumped out of the truck. "Come on, you!" Two bullets tore from his gun and plunged into Evan's chest.

Evan screeched in pain and disappeared over the hood.

"No!" slipped from Lana's trembling lips as she watched in horror; the thought of losing him again was devastating. "Evan." She wanted to run to him, help him; however, she was unable to move. Her body lay limp and the back of her head was bleeding. Tears blurred her already distorted vision and she placed her trembling hands to her face.

Suddenly, Evan bound through the air and landed atop Spence as he fired off one shot after another, sending two more bullets ripping through Evan's rigid skin. His gun clicked empty and he fought back with his fists.

"Evan!" Lana cried.

Screeching with rage, Evan dropped to the ground as

blood poured from his wounds and he fought to catch his breath.

"See, monster! You should know better than ta mess with Spence Rodgers!" Spence swiped an arm across his sweated brow.

Evan remained on the ground trying to regain his strength while listening to the words Spence shouted of his claim to glory.

"You're weak, nothing but a mere insect that needs to be crushed! And, your female will be mine to do as I wish." In three quick strides, Spence was beside Evan and kicked him. "Do you hear me, monster?"

Suddenly, Evan bound to his feet and webbing shot from his spinnerets. It quickly encased Spence, wrapping the entirety of his body from the neck down. Evan speedily scrambled to where Spence writhed within the cocoon; and biting down, he dug his fangs deep within Spence's skin. Flesh tore from bone and Spence screamed out in pain. His breath rushed from his body and blood poured from his wound.

Evan took another bite.

Spence shook and his shrieking screams turned into an assemblage of howls and indistinguishable moans, calls of the wild that Evan was somehow able to understand while in his present black widow form. Spence's appearance began to change, transform into something indescribable. And, the cocoon that he was encased in rapidly began to tear open. A beast, nearly identical to Evan's arachnid form, suddenly lunged into the open. Its screeching roar tore through the unsettled dust and it's gaze cut to Evan as it charged.

Lana had been holding her breath. "Oh my god!" she breathed. "He's a spider too!"

A battle between the two creatures began.

"Damn!" Trey hollered out as he quickly slowed the car to a halt behind Spence's truck. "There are two of those things now!"

Ignoring his friend's remark, Ches jumped out of the vehicle and raced toward the passenger door of the truck. Flinging Lana's door open, he caught her mid air.

"Hold on, sweetie; we'll get you outta' here." She groaned in pain as Ches glanced over at the two black widow spiders fighting, then turned back and shouted to Trey. "Trey, step it up, man. This girl needs medical attention."

Trey hurried around the front of his car and opened the passenger door and Ches slid in with Lana on his lap. Closing the door, Trey then quickly ran back around to the driver's side, climbed in and stomped on the gas.

"Go! Go! Go!" Ches shouted as Trey spun the car around and headed in the opposite direction.

Trey then glanced in his rearview mirror. Through the plume of dust, he could see the large black masses, their silver strands of webbing shooting through the air at lightening speed. Their monstrous bodies collided with one another, as each possessed the strength of an elephant, and the uncanny sound of barbaric screeching rang above the sound of the car's motor. "Ho-ly shit, there's two of 'em," he spoke beneath his breath.

"Whadya say?" Ches asked his friend.

"Nothing. I just said that we need to get her to a hospital."

Lana stirred slightly within Ches's arms and her head rested against his chest. This was the first feeling of comfort she had experienced in days and the thought of moving, leaving this fraction of semi-asylum, was unimaginable. Her mind refused to function correctly, rationalize the fact that Spence was now also a black widow. She shifted through the events that had occurred in the past several days in the attempt to find an answer. Her thoughts finally settled on the day he had abducted her, pulled her from the water and had tasted her blood. Her blood—was that it; Spence was now black widow because he had tasted her blood?

"Oh, Evan," she mumbled lowly.

Ches and Trey looked at her.

"What'd ya' say sweetheart?" Ches brushed a clump of matted hair away from her battered face. It was sticky with blood.

Lana's large brown eyes, which were gentle pools of grievous pain, met his. They pleaded for freedom from the aching discomfort and worry for Evan.

"Please, take me back."

"What?" Ches studied her eyes and tried to follow her trembling lips. "What did you say?"

Her head dropped back against his shoulder and her eyes were now closed. "Please," she whispered, "take me back."

They were now traveling on the main road leading into Billet; the hospital was another forty minutes away in Aune'.

Ches looked at the young girl that lay in his arms. Rage at what had been done to her boiled beneath his skin and he knew his friend felt the same. More than anything, he would have liked to pulverize Spence—drill him into the ground—him and that entire crew of his. However, the girl's welfare was priority.

"Do you think she's delirious? She is really messed up," Trey remarked as he watched her slip in and out of consciousness.

"You have to go to the hospital," Ches gently touched her cheek. "You've been hurt pretty bad and you may need some stitches in your head."

"Please." Lana's petite fingers trembled against his hand that held her firmly against his body. "Take me back. You can't take me to the hospital." Her words were strained. "They'll find out what I—"

Suddenly, the Charger was shoved from the rear and spun in the middle of the road. Trey whipped the wheel around in the attempt to keep the car from flipping and they came to a sudden stop.

"What the hell?" he exclaimed, though he knew the answer. It was one of the creatures coming for Lana. He looked over at Ches who was drawing his knife and peering through the cloud of dust beyond the windshield.

"Gah!" Trey suddenly jumped as Evan lunged at the vehicle. He was enormous, a charcoal-colored figure covered in millions of miniscule hairs and blood. His body and head were hideous, in frightening forms of the arachnid, with glowing red eyes that shifted between anger and confusion. He tilted his head slightly looking from Lana to the vehicle's other passengers. They remained like statues.

Lana's heart was breaking as the desire to be with Evan was overwhelming. She gently placed her hand on the passenger window and whispered his name, "Evan."

The beast roared and watched her through the glass.

"Let me out," she spoke quietly.

Ches looked over at Trey whose brows were high in his bangs and shoulders were arched exaggeratedly. Ches then took Lana's hand in his, "I don't think we should. You're already injured badly and you're liable ta' get hurt."

Lana's eyes never left those of the beast; and her mounting love for him gave her a minute amount of strength, strength to go to him and embrace him. She watched as his large red eyes slowly discontinued their blistering glow and gradually turned from crimson to golden brown. "Evan." The sound of his name was like an angel's breath. "I'm coming out."

Ches opened her door and she lowly groaned as she shifted her body in determination to move.

As if in understanding, the beast dropped to the ground, exhausted from his plight and the battle he had fought. Blood streamed from his wounds and he had grown weak. "*Lana,*" slipped from the creature's orifice— the boy within was calling her name.

"Where do you think the other one is?" Ches asked no one in particular; his eyes never leaving Evan. There was only open road and a few trees nearby.

"Hopefully dead," Trey replied acidly.

Lana slid from Ches's lap; she wobbled uneasily as her feet settled on the ground. Ches held her firmly around the waist, his strong grip making sure she didn't fall. She touched his arm as if silently saying she would be okay. He regretfully took his hands away.

Chapter 21

Lana gingerly stepped from within Ches's grip. The beast lay before her feet, staring up at her with eight eyes that were wide, deep pools of conflict. They gradually reverted from a fiery rage to a melancholy nature, portraying a lonely creature seeking refuge and comfort. His breathing was erratic, jagged spurts of broken air. Lana watched his huge chest, the mountainous figure, his thorax, rise and fall. The attractive human she knew with satiny chestnut-colored hair and beautiful kaleidoscopic eyes was hidden beneath the hard exterior of the beast and yearned to escape. She could feel his presence—comprehend his need to be free.

"Evan?" Tears streamed her cheeks. She had briefly forgotten the agonizing pain her body was in, the broken and severed arachnid limbs, her bruised and cut face and her fractured skull. The pain in her heart was twice what anything physical could inflict.

Trey slowly opened his door and climbed out. "Be careful." He edged toward the front of the car. Ches climbed out also.

Lana carefully bent and placed her hand upon Evan's

head. It was much smaller in comparison to the rest of his body. Two poisonous fangs jutted from the oddly shaped orifice and two feelers twitched methodically sensing the arachnid nature of Lana through her blood and the vibrations tingling his hairs.

Evan's body began to transform; and, Trey and Ches watched in amazement as the metamorphose slowly changed him from a hideous beast to an ordinary human.

Suddenly, Spence attacked as the metallic strands shot from the spinnerets within his abdomen and trapped Evan within his webbing. Evan was weak and his body was injured badly; and, in human form, he was meager prey to Spence's immense power and strength.

Ches immediately placed his body between Lana and the beast and hurriedly got her back inside the car. Then, he reached in the glove box and removed another knife, twice the size of the one he had been carrying. Meeting Trey at the front of the car, he donned a blade in each hand.

"Whatdaya' wanna' do?" Ches asked as he glanced back at Lana making certain she was safe. She clutched the dashboard to steady herself; her wide eyes met his. They were full of fear and trepidation which were clearly displayed in their unspoken plea for help, help for Evan who was so desperately losing the battle.

"I'm goin' in," Ches then announced.

Trey's brows resembled a bowtie; he was shocked at his buddies commandeering decision. Not that Ches allowed others to lead him around by a leash. It was just that Ches was normally laid-back, stress-free and less decisive. Trey attributed his friend's change in demeanor to the girl's presence. He readily obliged. "Okay. Let's do it!"

Ches charged Spence and in several strides had rapidly sliced through the long strands of webbing that were linking him to Evan. Spence screeched in rage and thundered toward them both.

"Oh no, you don't," Trey spun, executing the perfect side kick upon Spence as Ches hurled his blade, striking the beast in the abdomen. Spence dropped to the ground and shrieked in pain.

Trey shouted over his shoulder, "Hurry and get him in the car! I'll hold this one off."

The beast roared in fury and rushed toward Trey. Again, he executed a series of perfect kicks and punches, allotting them just enough time to escape.

"Hold on." Ches picked Evan up, flung him over his shoulder, then headed for the vehicle. Evan lowly moaned as his eyes closed and his body went limp. Ches ran for the car.

"Go! Go! Go!" He shouted as Trey jumped in the

driver's seat and slammed the gas to the floor. The car fishtailed and raced out onto the road. Spence followed.

Trey glanced down at the speedometer; they were traveling at 70mph and the beast was easily keeping pace. Its eight powerful spider legs scurried along the asphalt as vibrant strands of webbing shot in every direction. The beast was attaching itself to various items along the road and moving at breakneck speed.

"Man, is that thing on steroids?" Trey tilted his cap and pressed on the gas; the car's speed reached 85mph. He then glimpsed in his rearview mirror at Evan lying in the back.

Ches looked at Lana resting in his lap. She had fallen unconscious again; all the strength she had remaining had been depleted when going to Evan. A few strands of her dark hair lay against Ches's arm which held her secure. He tightened his grip on her then turned his attention back to the creature that was close behind.

A car passed them going in the opposite direction and slammed on its brakes. Without missing a stride, the beast cleared it and continued to charge in their direction. It moved as a freight train, barreling along the road at top speed.

"I can't outrun him on this crappy road! Any ideas?"

Ches thought for a moment and then replied, "Yeah. When I say turn, you turn. And, make it left. Turn left!"

Another vehicle passed them, blew its horn at Spence and slid into a ditch. Trey's charger scaled a knoll and thumped to the other side. A tractor trailer was headed in their direction; its load was light and it motored along at a tremendous speed. Ches increased his hold on Lana and braced himself. The tractor trailer raced closer and closer; it was now only three car lengths away.

"Turn now! Turn left now!"

Trey jammed on the brakes, yanked the steering wheel to the left, and cut in front of the truck. Spence had just crested the knoll and readily shot after the car. The truck horn blared as the driver slammed on the brakes and the large rig began to skid. It twisted sideways in a jackknife and suddenly slammed into Spence.

Trey pulled the car into a bay of the two-car garage and parked. Ches's black Jeep Wrangler sat in the other bay. They were at the house where he and Ches lived. It was a large house, consisting of living room, kitchen, three bedrooms, two bathrooms, basement and garage. They rented it at a decent rate from Trey's aunt while both he and Ches were attending college.

Trey laid his head on the steering wheel and sat quietly for a minute; he was pondering the situation.

"What do we do now?" Ches asked. He suddenly

realized he had been stroking Lana's hair; he quickly pulled his hand away.

Trey answered, pretending he hadn't noticed his buddy's actions. "Well, the girl was right; we couldn't have taken them to the hospital. We'll just haveta' take them inside and see about getting them some medicine and bandages for their wounds." Then, his demeanor became serious, his silken blue eyes evaluating the waves of emotion filling the vehicle. He looked at Ches.

"You *do* realize that's her boyfriend in the back?" It was more a direct statement than a question.

Ches just gazed at the many items flooding the garage: the dirt bikes, the surf boards, and the additional fishing equipment aside from what was now tossed haphazardly in the trunk and backseat. Without replying, he opened his door, shifted Lana's weight and carried her into the house.

Trey sighed heavily and shook his head. He then climbed out and drug Evan from the back of the car. Evan whispered Lana's name.

"She's okay; we'll take good take of her," Trey replied. Then, he hoisted Evan onto his shoulder; Evan groaned.

"So, *he* takes the pretty girl and leaves me with the guy wrapped in a cocoon. That's great, Ches." Slowly making his way inside, he headed to the living room and laid Evan on the couch.

Ches had taken Lana into his room and laid her on his bed. It was a king-sized bed, simple in décor with navy-colored sheets and matching silk comforter. And, there was a mound of pillows, all nearly the color of his eyes. The adorning bureau was dark walnut; he looked into the mirror and ran a hand through his blonde hair; it was disheveled and he looked tired.

Ches returned to Lana's side and briefly watched her. Then, deciding on the best medical treatment, he went into his adjoining bathroom for supplies.

Trey hollered in to him, "Hey, Ches, I'm outta' bandages, ya' have any extra?"

"Sure," Ches replied. His mind was miles away as he grabbed an extra box of gauze and tape and went into the living room.

Ches walked over to where Trey stood by the couch. They quietly observed Evan as he, lowly moaning, spoke Lana's name in a whisper. His dark hair was wet and his face glistened with sweat. The rest of his body was still encased in the webbing cocoon.

"So, who should we work on first?" Trey asked.

"Well, how about the guy; I think he's worse off." Ches pointed to a crimson spot growing on the cocoon. "He was shot a couple times and he must be bleeding pretty bad. It looks like it's soaking the threads."

"Welp, since you got to carry the girl in, buddy, I

vote *you* open the webbing," Trey winked.

Ches scowled. "I guess he's naked in there."

"Yep, I imagine so," Trey replied sheepishly. "Well, this should make it easier." He handed Ches a pair of wire cutters he had grabbed on his way in from the garage. "In the meantime, I'll check on the girl." He then turned and headed toward Ches's bedroom. "Oh and, Ches," Trey tossed him a blanket from a reclining chair, "ya' might need this."

Ches shot his friend a reproachful glare, then looked from the wire cutters and throw, he held, to Evan in his cocoon. He decided to grab some water and bath towels before he started cutting the webbing away. A basket of unfolded laundry sat just outside his bedroom door; he grabbed the towels from there and went to the kitchen for water.

"Evan?" Lana's small voice came from Ches's bedroom. She was steadying herself against its doorway. Trey was right behind her gently supporting her waist.

"She wanted to see him," Trey stated apologetically, possibly more for Ches's benefit than anything else. He helped Lana to the couch and she sat on the edge. Her face was puffed in spots, bruised and cut in others. She looked as if she had just been in a severe car accident and should be lying in the hospital.

"Evan?" Her trembling fingers touched his cheek, then she brushed a lock of damp hair from his forehead. His eyes fluttered lightly and he groaned in pain. "Can you help him?" Her eyes and voice were pleading as she glanced between Ches and Trey.

Trey tilted his hat back then placed a hand on her shoulder. "We'll try, but you may not wanna' be here."

"No, I'll stay."

After forty minutes of cutting the webbing, cleaning and bandaging Evan's wounds, Trey removed his cap and wiped his moistened brow. Lana was propped upright in the recliner. She had attempted to remain awake; however, as they had removed Evan's webbing and she had kept her eyes closed, she had succumbed to sleep.

"What about the girl's wounds?" Trey asked.

Ches had already been gathering Lana in his arms. He was headed toward his bedroom. "We'll let her rest for now. When she wakes up, we'll see how extensive her wounds are."

"Ches." Trey caught his friend by the arm.

Ches pulled his arm away. "I know." He went into his room and laid Lana on the bed. He covered her with the quilt and then headed into the bathroom for a shower; he needed to clear his head.

Night had settled quickly, bringing with it a heavy layer of clouds and a downpour of rain. Ches listened to the monotone of drops as they drummed upon the roof and raced along the gutter. The lights were dimmed and he sat in a chair watching the shadows play along the walls, and also watching Lana, as she tossed and turned in her sleep. Occasionally she cried out; it was always for Evan.

Trey had gone to bed several hours earlier after checking Evan's bandages and locking all the doors. The possibility of Spence still being alive had crossed each of their minds; however, neither had mentioned it.

"Evan?" Lana mumbled in her sleep. Ches went to her side and sat next to her on the bed. Retrieving the washcloth from the nightstand, he gently dabbed it along her forehead. Her eyes slowly opened and she momentarily gazed into his face.

"How's Evan?" she whispered as she pushed herself up on her elbows.

"He's fine," Ches replied. "Banged up pretty good, but fine." Lana's hand touched his.

"Thank you."

"You're welcome." He brushed away the strands of hair that silhouetted her face. "Are you in much pain?"

She blinked her enormous dark eyes. "No. I'm feeling quite better thank you." She placed her fingers to her face and touched her skin. It no longer felt swollen and the cuts had become just tiny puckers. Her puffy lips had even returned to normal.

"Lana." This was the first time Ches had said her name. It sent an odd, yet splendid feeling flowing through his body. A feeling he hadn't felt for years. "We were wondering how Evan would have taken all those gunshots and still have lived. Plus, your wounds have healed while you slept. Does that have anything to do with both of you transforming?"

She answered quietly, "I guess so. Things have happened so quickly and every time I start crying, I turn into…that…that…thing." She became silent and her large brown eyes clouded over and filled with tears. The large droplets slipped between her heavy black lashes and slid down her cheeks. "I don't know what's happening."

Ches wrapped his arms around her and held her close. Her slight body trembled against his muscular form and her warm tears moistened his shirt. "My parents are dead, my brother is missing and …" Her crying grew to hiccupping sobs. "And, now I'm, I'm a…

"Lana?" Evan was supporting himself against the door frame, wrapped in the quilt Trey had covered him with. His kaleidoscopic eyes flared from hazel to black, then, to red. The beast within him fumed with irritation and fury. His gaze was focused on Ches and her and he wobbled unsteadily. "What are you doing?"

"Evan!" Lana quickly pulled from Ches's embrace. She suddenly felt conscious of her inadvertent actions.

The color drained from Evan's red cheeks and his head dropped to his chest. He suddenly slid to the floor.

"Oh, my gosh!" Lana hurried to where he lay. She touched his burning forehead then glanced back at Ches who was right behind her. "What's the matter with him? He's burning up!"

"I don't know," Ches replied as he lifted Evan and secured his arm around his waist. He helped Evan back into the living room and onto the couch. Then, he retrieved a wet cloth from the kitchen and returned to place it on Evan's forehead. "Maybe he should go to the hospital."

"No!" Lana whispered. "You can't take him there!" She recalled what had happened at the military base and how she and her brother had been treated. "They'll do all sorts of testing there. And..." she suddenly blurted out... "They killed my parents!"

Lana dropped to her knees and gripped the edge of the couch as tears raced to her eyes and she hid her face.

Ches bent and placed his arm around her. "It's okay. We won't take him." He took her chin in his hand and gently turned her face toward him. His azure-colored eyes gazed into hers and his smile, glowing in the dim lighting, was as warm as the rays of the afternoon sun. He was kind and gentle and his words were reassuring. "I promise."

Lana smiled half-heartedly, feeling somewhat assured. She immediately noticed that the webbing that normally grew from the hour-glass shaped mark upon her stomach when she was upset hadn't started.

"I'm sorry we've been so much trouble," she whispered.

"Oh, don't worry about it," he grinned at her. "It's my pleasure."

Suddenly, her body felt grungy and she was exhausted. Wiping her tears with the back of her hand, she slowly stood to her feet. "I was wondering if I could take a shower." She fingered the strands of her sticky hair.

"Of course," Ches remarked. "You can use my shower." He grabbed a wash cloth and towel from the clothes basket and walked her through his room to the bathroom door. "Here ya' go." He handed her the items. "There's soap and shampoo in there already; and, if you need anything else just let me know."

Ches turned to see Trey leaning against the door. His arms were crossed and his gaze narrowed. "I just came ta' check on ya', buddy."

"What? Are you my wet-nurse now?"

"No," Trey replied. "But, I do intend on keeping you from drowning."

"Then just throw me a rope and stay outta' my room."

Trey put his hands in the air, a signal he was surrendering. "*Okay*, but your cookies will burn if you don't remove them from the oven."

Ches scowled and looked at his friend. "You and your clichés; since when do you care about my cookies burning?"

"After seeing you burn a whole batch." Trey grinned.

"Oh, shut up you pansy." Ches picked up his boot and tossed it at his friend. "Go bake your cookies somewhere else."

Trey chuckled and disappeared out the door. His voice floated back into the room. "So, don't go blamin' me when your kitchen's burned."

Ches rolled his eyes. He then turned his attention back to Lana. The water was running; she was already in the shower. He placed his hand on the door then leaned against it with his forehead. "What am I doing?" The empty space in his heart was gradually being filled with a need and a want, a desire to be close to this girl—this girl who transformed into something other than just a woman. He believed in love at first sight; it had struck him once before like a tornado ravaging a town.

Ches clenched his fists and left the room.

Chapter 22

THREE DAYS LATER

Evan dreamt he was seven again. He was attending a ball game with his father who sat beside him on the bleachers. It was the fourth inning and their team was winning. He glanced over at his father who was laughing and clapping his hands. It was one of the most joyous days in Evan's life. However in the distance, dark clouds slowly began to rumble along the sky and a crack of lightning raced to meet the ground. The sky suddenly grew dark and the ball players had all packed up and left for home. His father, who had been smiling and enjoying the game, was no longer there. Evan was all alone. *Father?* He called to him. *Where are you?*

A spider raced along his leg just below where his shorts met his knee. He screeched and brushed it away. Suddenly, there were more; they were crawling over his entire body and he screamed out for help.

Evan awoke in a panic. His body was drenched with sweat and his breathing was coming in spurts. He groaned as he sat up and looked around; the digital clock on the wall read 6:02 a.m. The morning sun was peeking through the slightly parted drapes bringing with it warm gentle rays that settled upon his face and skin. He tried to recall where he was. The living room he was in was enormous, larger than his living room and kitchen put together. It was decorated moderately with couch, recliner, stereo, television and a shelf full of books, DVDs and CDs.

The fight with Spence slowly filtered into Evan's foggy mind, along with their escape and them arriving here; here, wherever this place was. He felt the bandages encasing his chest. Then, suddenly, he remembered seeing Lana in bed, embraced in the arms of someone else. Anger raged inside him and he winced at its intensity. He struggled to his feet; and though his nightmare was gone, his body still boiled hot and he ached immensely. He groaned as he made his way to the nearby clothesbasket for something to wear. A pair of jeans and t-shirt he dug out of the basket was nearly a perfect fit; he carefully slipped them on over his bandages.

"Evan?" Lana appeared in the doorway of Ches's room. Her dark hair accentuated the milky whiteness of her creamy complexion and the fullness of her large dark eyes. The long chestnut-colored ringlets cascaded around her face and fell along her petite shoulders and the long over-sized white shirt she wore. Evan had to catch his breath. She looked lovely.

"What are you doing?" she asked softly.

Evan laboriously tore his eyes away. He didn't answer. The fury at what he had seen enraged the beast within him, made it nearly impossible to breathe. He temporarily forgot about his injuries; and, without answering, he turned and made his way toward the front door.

"Evan?" Lana hurried to where he stood and gently touched his arm. His skin was hot, as if a fire were raging rampant within his body. And, his eyes which were normally gentle and kind were cold and steely; they sent a shiver running along her skin. "Please, answer me."

"Lana? Is something wrong?" Ches emerged from within his room; he was dressed only in jeans. His hair was mussed and sleep was heavy in his eyes. He scratched the back of his neck. "What's goin' on?"

"Nothing!" Evan snapped. His eyes blazed near black. He looked at Lana for a moment then turned and walked out the door.

Evan quickly transformed and headed for home. His injuries began to heal swiftly, assisted by his metamorphose. Now, he would need to feed. A female black widow along with her sack of eggs, and a screeching crow were absorbed within his webbing, liquefied and ingested. They would suffice for now.

The injuries and scars had disappeared; however, the heated burning of human flesh remained as he fought the beast that wanted to consume him, keep him a hideous monster forever. However, he continually fought the transformation his body insisted on, had fought it for the past few days while he wanted nothing more than to remain human, human like the two who had come to his and Lana's rescue. He fought the creature, struggled with its empowering control as it seemed to be consuming him lately due to his anger and rage. He knew it had to do with Lana, the arachnid female—his female.

It didn't take long for Evan to arrive at the cabin. He had moved rapidly through the surrounding forest; wanting to rid himself of this horrid form, break free of its curse. He metamorphosed quickly, then grabbed the shorts from the outside hook, slipped them on and went inside. He knew Diana was there. She rushed to embrace him.

"Oh, Evan!" She smiled wide and her sapphire-colored eyes danced with excitement behind her fading bruises. She held him close, happily absorbing the warmth of his bronze body. She nestled her face in the soft curve of his neck. He had never been this hot before; his skin was normally very cool to the touch.

He scowled and slowly pushed her away. "Please, Diana, not now."

She slowly backed away. Her dancing eyes lost their tempo and her enthusiastic smile disappeared. She then turned, walked over and sat on the couch. Resting her chin on her hand, she stared at the wall. Her lower lip jutted beneath her upper.

Evan knew the pouting would begin shortly. After all these years, he had grown accustomed to her pouting when she didn't get her way. However, he did feel guilty for hurting her feelings.

He walked over and sat next to her on the couch. He sighed. "Look, I'm sorry."

Diana turned toward him. His body was hot; it radiated like a fire from his skin. "I knew somethin' was terribly wrong with ya'll the minute I hugged ya'." She touched his chest. "The heat comin' from ya'll's skin nearly melted my brassiere off." She smiled wide and her eyes twinkled. Understanding rekindled upon her face. "So, that's what's wrong with lil' ol' you; ya'll have a fever. I'll git ya' a cool wash cloth."

Diana hurried away and disappeared into the bathroom before he could even respond. Evan was just grateful she wasn't moping; it would have only added to his aggravation. She returned quickly and dabbed the cool cloth along his forehead, then she proceeded to run it gently along his burning chest. Her long hair swept along his bare legs. It slightly tickled and he shifted in his seat.

"Why ya'll so hot?" she asked. Her tone was low, almost a whisper. She moved slightly closer to him and her cherry scented breath wafted upon his face. It smelled nice, refreshing and her blonde waves brushed against his heated skin. The cool washcloth disappeared behind his neck along with her arm. She was nearly sitting in his lap.

Evan shook his head and abruptly rose to his feet. "I really need something to drink." He went into the small kitchen and filled a glass with water. He downed it quickly then filled another and did the same. Diana was right behind him.

"I'm sorry, Evan." She gently turned him to face her. "I've just bin worried sick about ya'll; that's all. Ya'll have been gone a few days and I missed ya'."

"Diana—" He began to say, but was suddenly interrupted by her cherry-scented lips. They pressed hard against his, passionately yearning and desiring him while melding the two as one. Her body pushed tightly against his bronze form; he was hot, scorching from the unknown fire that burned within. He suddenly couldn't breath.

"Diana!" he scolded mildly, "I'm sick." It was partially a lie, yet partially truth. He quickly grabbed her hands that were gripping at his body in a maddening haste; he backed away from her. "You'll catch what I have."

"I don't care!" she mewled. "I was so afraid ya'll was with that Lana girl. I can't stand the thought of you and her together!" Her voice and eyes were pleading, deep blue pools of ache and frustration. They longed for him, basked in the heated warmth of his body and the flecks of his stunning dark eyes.

"I love you!" she blurted out. "I've always loved ya!"

Evan held tightly to her hands then moved his grasp to her shoulders. He gazed into her eyes; they were lovely, a bouquet of violets blooming in the summer sun; they worshiped him, remained true to only him.

Diana stood on her toes and slowly but gently placed her mouth to his. She parted her lips and kissed him long and passionately, her cherry-scented breath coming in spurts. For the first time, Evan kissed her back.

Her hands grasped his bare chest and knitted at his skin like a new-born kitten. Leaping into his arms, she wrapped her long legs around his waist and pressed her body against his. His skin was hot; blazing to the touch, and, the heat seeping from his body was flowing into hers. It rushed like a tidal wave through her blouse and skirt, causing her to sweat.

Evan easily carried her to the living room. The dim lighting glimmered and glowed, casting dancing shadows upon the wall, as they appeared to be lovers on a moonlight night.

Evan carefully laid her slender body upon the couch. The long locks of her honey-blonde hair cascaded about her and her bright eyes blinked. Her heart was pounding in her chest and she smiled in mild apprehension, yet warranted certainty. Evan knew that this was what she had wanted from the day she snuck into his house.

He heard her breath slip from her red lips as he lay on top of her. She was beautiful and her soft white skin was silky and fresh, scented with vanilla. She was any man's dream.

Evan nestled his face in her hair, drawing in the scented mixture of her body's sweat and the fragrance she wore. It was tantalizing to his human nature and torturous to the creature within a struggle of man versus beast. She wrapped her arms around him and pulled him close. Her lips brushed against the curvature of his neck and her cool breath was like ice against his heated skin.

"Evan." She whispered into his ear and the dark ringlets of his hair. "I'm yours forever."

Forever, the word echoed in his mind and remained in the recesses of his emotional intellect. *She* would be his forever, until time stood still and all mankind had disappeared. *But how*, he wondered. He was a beast, something she was not; and, he would live for forever—for eternity—and she would not.

Suddenly, he thought of Lana. *She* would live forever, forever with her curse, a curse she may never be able to control. A clear image of her wrapped in her own webbing filled his mind. Then another with her and a hundred arachnid babies which were also wrapped in their own webbing. He laughed inside at the ridiculous thought. Then suddenly, out of nowhere, an ache rushed to his heart. And though his flesh was burning and this beautiful female lay beneath him, his heart was empty and he yearned for someone else— someone who had been in the arms of another. The beast within him blazed with fury, burned for the girl who was no longer with him.

Diana's mouth was now frantically searching every inch of Evan's firm bronze chest.

"Diana." He spoke her name with slight urgency.

"*Oh, Evan*," she breathed through a panted breath. Her lips continued to search his upper body then every crevice of his neck.

"Diana." He gently grabbed her face and held her chin in his hand. Her sapphire eyes were clouded with desire and her breath came sporadically. Strands of long, streaked, blonde hair hung haphazardly around her beautiful face which was spattered with droplets of sweat. Her southern drawl was thick and choked as she spoke. "What, Evan honey?"

"I can't," he responded evenly. Then, his voice became more pressing. "I can't do this."

Confusion riddled her lovely features and she blinked her eyes. *"What?"*

He pushed himself off her and sat within the vice-like grip of her legs. "I said, *I can't do this.*" His eyes avoided her gaze, the hurt that was extinguishing the spark in her eyes.

Diana quickly sat up and attempted to collect herself and smooth her disheveled clothing and hair. Her mind was clearing and she thought with a bit of clarity. Her voice was edged. "What are ya'll saying, Evan?"

He untangled himself from her legs and stood up then took a few steps toward the front door. Unable to meet her stricken gaze, he kept his back toward her. "I think you should go home."

"Why?" she asked, a plead surmounting her

southern drawl. "I've saved myself for ya'll all these years. Aren't I desirable to ya'?" She slid her feet to the floor and stood. "Look at me!" Desperation touched her voice.

Evan slowly turned. His eyes ran from her stricken face to her flawless body. She had the face of an angel, yet the delectability of Satan's forbidden fruit. Her breasts were perfect, large and perky; and her shapely torso and perfect flat stomach disappeared within her tight skirt. Her legs were long, smooth as silk; they made the entire package tall and willowy, drinkable. Diana was beautiful; the most beautiful girl he had ever seen next to Lana.

"Ya'll are thinkin' of that Lana girl, aren't ya'."

He didn't answer. He couldn't speak.

Diana's hurt expression immediately turned irate and accusatory. "What? Were ya'll with her? Did ya'll take her?" In two deliberated strides, Diana stood before him. "I've saved myself fer' ya'. Just fer you!"

Suddenly, she drew back and punched him in the mouth. Tears burst to her eyes like waves crashing along the shore; they rolled down her quivering cheeks. "I hate you, Evan LaBonte!" She hurried to the door and angrily threw it open. Then, she was gone.

Chapter 23

Lana sniffled and buried her face in the pillow on Ches's bed. "Evan, why did you leave me here?" she mumbled. She lay curled up on her side facing away from the bedroom door; it was closed and the curtains were drawn. Darkness filled the room though the light of day shone brightly outside. Lana looked at the clock on the nightstand. It read 10:31 a.m.

She could hear Ches and Trey's faint utterances coming from just outside the bedroom door. Their harsh whispers indicated that a disagreement was in progress. Wiping her moistened eyes, she rolled over and listened closely.

"I warned you about this." She recognized Trey's voice. It wasn't as soft or reserved as Ches's.

"Look, Trey," Ches's voice was calm, almost too calm, "I want her to stay here with me."

Lana blinked and quickly sat up. "What? Is he talking about *me*? He wants *me* to stay *here*?" She frantically searched her mind while Ches and Trey's mutterings were just background clamor to her galloping thoughts. A few moments passed and a soft knock sounded upon the door; it cracked open and Ches peeked inside.

"May I come in?" His voice was gentle, yet it remained reserved. The wonderful smell of eggs and bacon cooking filled her nostrils. Her stomach growled.

Lana was still in the oversized nightshirt he had lent her; she practically swam in it. She quickly covered her bare legs with the large quilt.

"Okay." Her voice cracked slightly. For some unknown reason, she suddenly felt queasy.

The door opened wide to allow his large frame inside. The room was dark and she was unable to see his expression clearly; though, she could partially see Trey standing in the lighted background behind him. Trey's brows were pressed together and his lips pursed. He looked as if he had something else to say. His gaze caught hers and he turned and walked away.

"May I open the curtains?" Ches abruptly asked.

Before Lana could stumble out an answer, he was tugging on a drawstring and they were sliding back on their tracks to greet the walls.

Lana blinked her eyes at the lights intensity and attempted to focus while Ches returned to stand beside the bed. Rubbing her eyes, she brought his form into focus. This was the first time she had looked at him clearly; it had always been from behind a wall of tears. He was tall and slightly brawnier than Evan; however, not by much. His face could be compared to that of an angel. His jaw was chiseled yet smooth and firm and his lips were full and perfect. Sun-bleached blonde hair, touched lightly by waves, and was streaked perfectly with shades of russet that outlined his face. It made him look young and boyish, yet grown and a man. He had beautiful blue eyes the color of sapphire stones, and a smile that brightened the room. He looked like he had just walked off the front cover of the modeling magazine, *Surfer*. Lana had to catch her breath; Ches was gorgeous. He looked at her strangely. Suddenly, she noticed her mouth had dropped open and she had been staring. The blood rushed to her cheeks and she quickly snapped her jaw closed and turned her head.

Ches laughed lightly at her reaction, then sat on the bed next to her. "Your blushing accentuates your lovely features. It's nice."

Lana glanced at him out of the corner of her narrowed eyes. "There isn't anything complimentary about one's mouth hanging open and staring. Basically, I think it's rude."

Ches laughed again, somewhat louder this time. Lana smiled in spite of herself.

"That's it. It's nice to see you smiling for once. I knew it was hidden in there." He softly touched her forehead with his large forefinger. She felt like a small child again—young and reliant.

He then continued. "I know you're still upset about Evan leaving; that's understandable. But, I just wanted to let you know that you're welcome to stay here. More than welcome," he added. His face had become statuesque as he awaited her answer; however, his crystalline eyes which sparkled with the late morning sun appeared somewhat apprehensive. Lana remained quiet and her heart pounded loudly in her chest. She was stunned by the abrupt situation she was suddenly put in.

Ches stood to his feet and ran a hand through his thick hair. "Well, you don't have to answer right now. I know a lot has happened in the past few days. However, I would ask that you think about it." He bent and took her slender hand. His mouth momentarily hovered above her alabaster skin as his warm breath and lips then gently brushed her knuckles. A quiver raced along Lana's spine and ended at her fingertips. Then, he was standing and disappearing into the bathroom.

It happened so quickly she hadn't realized she had been holding her breath. She exhaled lightly and watched as he reappeared and opened the double doors to his closet. He diligently searched the small area. Then, the doors rolled on their metal tracks and closed with a mild bang. He then returned to the bedside and handed

Lana a neatly folded skirt and sweater. "Here," he said, "you can wear these; they belonged to someone very special." Sadness touched his eyes and he smiled in spite of it. "Oh, and Trey and I made some food. You've gotta' be hungry." Leaving the room, he closed the door behind him.

Lana carefully unfolded the two garments he had handed her. The skirt was long and soft, light in fabric, a peasant skirt. It was lovely with multi-shades of the deepest russets and brilliant shades of gold. White miniscule sequined flowers played upon the two ruffled layers; they danced like diamonds in the sun's beaming light.

Excitement taunted Lana's girlish emotions and she eagerly reached for the other garment. Its fabric was also very light; but, unlike the skirt, it was silky, delicate to the touch and the most wonderful shade of burgundy—red wine poured directly from a bottle. The sleeves were three quarter length and a small delicate ruffle accentuated the fine neckline. Lana couldn't wait to put them on.

Colette placed the slice of white bread on top the bologna and squashed the sandwich she was making with her hand. A small piece of stale crust crumbled to the counter top.

"Shut up, you mangy mutts!" The dogs had been rowdy the entire morning—incessantly barking their foolish heads off. She tossed the knife oozing with extra mayonnaise into the sink. It clanged loudly as it bounced off the pile of dishes that were food encrusted and had been sitting in the sink for days. She wasn't washing them. This was Spence's place, not hers. She just hung out here after she had grown tired of her parent's nagging and also when she felt ornery and needed to hang out with someone equivalent to her vile, despicable self. She touched the mound of bandages taped across her nose. Her nose was broken—broken in two places. She grumbled loudly and slammed her narrow fist on the edge of the sink. The dilapidated counter shook and the dirty dishes rattled.

It had been three days since Spence had left with the mutated girl; and the two, so-called cowboys, had torn out after them. She didn't care; she was more pissed about her nose; and, if an opportunity arose for payback, she would be the first to inflict it.

Colette grumbled again and angrily took a bite of her sandwich. The dogs continued their barking; it was adding to her irritation and escalating headache.

In three quick strides she was at the front door and yanking it open. She shoved the screen door wide and it cracked against the siding of the trailer. *"Shut up..."*

Her voice trailed off and her emerald eyes narrowed, sparked with undivided interest at the object that had Spence's two German Shepherds in a rash of hysteria. The sandwich dropped from her hand and she cleared the steps without a thought. The sound of her own screaming rang in her ears as she raced across the dirt-encrusted yard. "Get back! Get away from him!" She waved her hands and kicked her slippered feet at them.

A creature lay on the ground before her, part human, part spider. She knew it was Spence; the upper torso was his, however the rest was a gross deformity, much worse than what the girl's had been. Plus, he was covered in blood; and bone, and flesh were exposed where they shouldn't be.

"Spence?" Colette extended her hand to him. "Spence, are you okay?" His leering topaz eyes glared up at her. He didn't answer. The long arachnid legs quivered uncontrollably moving him slowly across the ground. They seemed to be dragging his distorted, partially crushed body.

The female German Shepherd, named Trixie, who was Spence's favorite, again moved closer while the other stood farther away, aloof to the situation, seeming if not bored. Trixie, slowly advanced on Spence's deformed figure with her tail tucked tight between her hind legs. She cautiously sniffed the blood caked to his arms and upper torso, his hair and face. Then, settling herself down next to him, she whimpered mildly and began to lick his wounds.

"Stop that, you stupid mutt!" Colette snapped. She turned to face Spence. "Spence, what do you want me to do?" She retrieved a previously piece of chewed gum from within her bra and popped it into her mouth. She made a face at the loss of flavor; then titling her head in a never-mind gesture, she blew a small bubble. Suddenly, Spence grabbed her bony ankle. She gasped and her hand flew to her chest.

"Quit with the damn gum chewing you wretched bimbo and help me in the house!" Colette immediately tucked her gum back inside her bra and scrambled to acquire one of his arms. He added, "Then, call the boys; we're gonna have a meeting."

The piece of firewood crackled as it separated and split in two then divided and fell like two wounded soldiers to meet the ground. Evan picked up another large piece and set it upright on the stump he used as a chopping block. Briefly, he leaned on the axe he was using and looked around; then, he swiped a gloved hand over the beads of sweat pasting his dark hair to his forehead and neck. Winter was right around the corner and the air was cool and crisp. Yet Evan was hot, hotter than usual.

He didn't feel ill, an urge to lie down and rest, or to see a doctor. What he did feel was: restless, irate, a surging charge rushing through his body like a crashing tidal wave—a tsunami. The arachnid beast within him thirsted for the enticing bouquet of Lana's scent, her blood—the arachnid female's smell that would allure any male black widow. And, his human emotions suffered nearly as much, while he fought desperately to forget her—forget her long flowing dark hair, large liquid eyes, tender voice that spoke his name, and her sweet flowery scent that gingerly filled his sensitive nostrils.

"What is wrong with me?" His mind shifted through the compilation of his thoughts like a professor shuffling through the many pages of a book. He couldn't remember ever feeling this way, this excessive struggle and pain that drove him to fits of rage then to periods of depression. He had always attempted to remain in control of his feelings, suppress the anger and hurt that he had been forced to manage since he was a young boy.

His mind drifted to the day his mother had been killed, *killed by him*, the arachnid beast. The pain he had felt then was wrenching, a great loss in the haze of a horrible nightmare, and yet somehow surmounted by his overpowering fear. Then, when Grandmother Hobbs had passed it was like losing his mother all over again. She had given him hope and courage, all those things a mother's love portrays, caring for him like a son. She had known of his existing disfigurement yet had loved him regardless.

Each time she left him in the cabin, it had ached him to see her go. The last day seemed to ache for an eternity.

"Evan, I'm going into the hospital tomorrow and I may not be returning."

"The hospital?" He had exclaimed. *"What for Grandmother? And, what do you mean, you won't be returning?"* He was preoccupied with gathering his notebook and pencil. *"Sure you will, I'll see you like always. You have to help me with my algebra."* His large kaleidoscopic eyes flashed playfully and he grinned crookedly as he joked, *"You're the only one who knows this brainiac stuff."*

Evan grabbed the algebra book off the kitchen counter and balanced it upon his head. *"Look what I've been practicing, Grandmother."* Then, he proceeded to place a full glass of water on top the book. He headed toward the living room where she was sitting on the couch. His back was straight and his arms were extended for balance. He glided awkwardly across the floor as he bit his tongue which peeked from the corner of his mouth.

Suddenly, he ducked down. The book and glass dropped, falling toward the floor, but Evan swiftly caught them both in mid-air. Not a drop of water had spilled and the book had landed safely in his outstretched hand. *"Tah dah!"* He bowed exuberantly then plopped down on the couch next to her.

Marianne smiled meekly and clapped; it wasn't her normal congratulatory, high-spirited clap that usually sent them dancing around the room and laughing until their stomach's hurt. She could barely crack a smile.

The axe angrily struck the oak log; it split in two and plummeted to the ground banging atop the others. Evan grabbed another piece of wood, steadied it, then swung again. The memories continued to flood his mind.

Marianne turned toward him, tears lay in the lower lids of her eyes. *"No, Evan. I don't think I'll be able to."*

The color had slipped from Evan's youthful face and his bright smile disappeared. He searched her eyes. They had aged and turned gray; and the tiniest sparkle, hidden in the kindling irises that portrayed her love of life and him, remained but came at a painful price.

"What do you mean? You have to come back." He watched every line of her face, more prominent than years passed. The branched lines that accentuated each of her eyes, the ones he was so familiar with, quivered

slightly and were etched deeper. And, the many others, she referred to as character lines, appeared suddenly to have increased in length and depth; time had taken its toll. A smile attempted unsuccessfully to reach the corners of her thin lips.

Evan could hear the sound of the wood splitting as it cracked and fell to the ground. His heart was racing the same as it had then.

Marianne continued. *"Something's wrong with this old ticker of mine."* She was unable to fight the anxiety that seeped through her eyes causing her voice to waver. Her lips quivered. *"I have to have surgery."* Her hands wrung together on her lap.

"Surgery!" Evan cried. *"But, people have surgery all the time! And, they go home."* His pleading eyes searched hers for an answer and he clenched his fists as his body mildly shook.

Marianne blinked her eyes; a miniscule glimmer of hope shielding them from the coming tears. *"We'll see."*

She then wrapped her arms around Evan and hugged him tightly. She knew her strength was waning as it had become difficult to just come out here to see him. Then, she abruptly pulled him away. Her face had become severe and her eyes set. *"However, promise me this, Evan Labonte."* Evan knew she was serious when she called him by his full name. *"Promise me you'll take every precaution we've discussed—every precaution to keep yourself safe."* She pulled a piece of paper from her jacket pocket and pressed it into his hand. *"I've been working with a young man by the name of Jacob Winslow. He knows of your secret and is willing to help you. If I don't come back within ten days, you can locate him at this address."* She closed his hand tightly around the small slip of paper.

Evan's entire body was numb; he never felt the small slip of paper as it crumpled in his clenched palm.

Marianne hugged him again; tighter this time. Then, she turned and headed toward the cabin door. Evan was stunned. His mind refused to wrap around what was happening. He couldn't form the words to express what he was feeling and his bare feet were rooted to the wooden floor. She opened the door and Hershey appeared before her. He wagged his tail slowly and licked her weathered hand. Marianne rubbed his head which had whitened through time. *"Now you take good care of Evan for me, Hersh."* The golden retriever, nearly the same age as she in dog years, seemed to understand. He slowly walked to Evan's side and lazily sat down.

Marianne glanced back at Evan, tears were now

uncontrollably streaming down her quivering cheeks. *"Good bye, Evan."* Then, she was gone.

Evan propped the axe against the stump and began to pick the pieces of wood up to stack them on the nearby pile. His thoughts then shifted to the encounters of the previous week. They abruptly settled on the picture of Lana in Ches's arms. "Damn it!" he shouted as he picked up the last piece of wood and flung it with all his might. It sailed through the trees and smacked a maple. The sound was like thunder, seeming to shake the entire forest.

Diana watched Evan the entire day through her small window. He had been splitting wood all day. She watched as his anger had escalated on occasion to an act of rage or violence—like hurling a piece of firewood or his axe. However, after several trips into the forest to look for the tool, he discontinued throwing the axe and just threw wood. Then, more-often-than-not, his rage would reduce to a simmering ache where he would look around with narrowed eyes as if he were watching for someone, waiting. Then, slumping his shoulders beneath his sweat-laden t-shirt, he would return to his chore. Diana ground her teeth. "Lana, I don't know what ya'll did ta' my Evan, but if I see ya'll again, I'm gonna' hurt you."

She grabbed a light sweater, slipped it on, then proceeded outside. The sun was shining brightly and wisps of white cottony clouds floated overhead, pressed forward by the chilled autumn air.

Evan's head snapped up at the sound of her front door clicking shut behind her. She had tried to escape the cabin undetected so as to not draw attention to herself before she was ready to rectify the situation between them. However, he must have heard the latch. She briefly wondered how. Then, before he could look away, she caught his gaze. She smiled sheepishly, recalling the last time she had been with him; that had been nearly a week ago. Her knuckles on her right hand still hurt. She rubbed them gingerly.

For the first time in her life, Diana's legs felt heavy, even after, on one occasion, she had hoggishly ingested an entire bag of chips, something she rarely ever did because of the fat and salt. Her face soured at the amount of grease she had licked from her fingers. "Ugh," she groaned.

Evan's eyes narrowed as he watched her approach. The sun's rays caught his irises prismatic colors of liquid gold and russet, chocolate browns and mocha; they sparkled with unexplained animation.

Diana now stood within a few feet from him. Her arms were tight across her front and her booted toe nudged at a small mound of dirt. The air between them was thick with tension as a million thoughts raced through her mind making it difficult to breathe. Never before had she felt so foolish, so out of control. Silently, she cursed Lana for causing this.

Evan set the axe down and turned to walk away. The whole situation had become too difficult, something he hadn't had to deal with in all the one hundred plus years he had lived on this earth. Maybe it was time for him *not* to exist, to escape this hell for something else; *but what*, he thought. What would be at the conclusion of his existence, if there was one? The thought increased his depression, he headed for the cabin.

"Evan!" Diana nearly screeched his name. "I...I need ta' talk ta' ya'll." She reached for his arm. Though he stopped mid-stride, he didn't look at her. Her voice slightly broke as she struggled for the correct words, words that would heal their relationship and return it to what it had been. "I'm sorry!" she blurted out. "I don't hate ya'll at all." Her voice nearly became a whisper as she glanced at the ground and nudged at the dirt some more. "In fact, I love ya'll more than anythin'."

He turned toward her and finally spoke. "Diana, you know I don't..." She placed her fingers to his warm lips.

"Sssh, please don't say it. I know ya'll don't love me." Her eyes met his and she fought the tears that clouded her vision while her heart was, without doubt, breaking in two like the wood he had split.

"I'm sorry." He took her chin in his gloved hand. The heat was seeping through the leather. It warmed her face. Then, he looked into her paining eyes. "I don't deserve someone like you."

Diana thought about that for a moment as she quietly shuffled through her thoughts. Then, she appeared to slightly perk up. "Ya'll are right." Then, blinking her eyes, she added. "I'm more like ya'll's sister. Right?" She seemed to be convincing herself in some odd, unfamiliar way.

"Yes," Evan affirmed as he hugged her gently. "My sister." Diana smiled as she pressed herself tightly against his heated body.

Chapter 24

Lana slowly opened the bedroom door and peeked into the living room. Ches stood there waiting, his bright smile was contagious as she stepped through the door. The clothing he had given her was a perfect fit and it complimented the darkness of her hair and eyes that contrasted her ivory skin.

Trey stood in the shadows behind Ches with his arms crossed and his brows furrowed. He quickly and quietly turned and headed toward the kitchen. A metal tray banged loudly against the stovetop and the oven door slammed closed. Ches frowned in Trey's direction; then he crossed the room in several strides and was by Lana's side.

"You look absolutely lovely." He gently took her hand and held her at arm's length. Turning her slowly, he marveled at her beauty. Lana blushed.

"Are you eating or not?" Trey's irritation resounded with the glass plates as they banged against the kitchen table.

"We're coming." Ches threw him an annoyed glance, then he looked back at Lana apologetically.

"I'm sorry about that. Trey isn't fond of having

company this long."

"That's not it, Ches." Trey called from the kitchen. A metal utensil rang sharply as it cracked against the table.

Lana studied Ches's face. His brows were drawn and his normally congenial demeanor seemed to have turned slightly annoyed.

"He doesn't want me here, does he?"

"No, no; that's not it," Ches struggled to find the right words while his thoughts were constructed around the ass-kicking he was going to give Trey later.

"Yes, that *is it*, Ches," Trey replied as he leaned against the wooden post that supported a partial partition between the living room and kitchen. He carefully held a piece of extra warm bacon between two fingers and nonchalantly took a bite. "I don't want you here." His gaze settled on Lana. The color immediately drained from her face.

"Trey! What the hell's the matter with you? Why would you tell her that?" Ches was quickly becoming irate.

Trey leaned his head back, opened his mouth and dropped the last piece of bacon into it.

"Welp, for one thing," he chewed, "three's a crowd." Swallowing, he reached behind the partition and grabbed another piece of bacon off a plate. "And, secondly…" he tossed it into his mouth, "There are others involved here." His blue eyes drilled into Ches's; they both knew he was referring to Evan.

Lana slowly released her grip from Ches's; her face was drawn and pale. "It's okay; I understand. I'll just find somewhere else to go." Before Ches could respond, she had disappeared into the bedroom and locked the door.

"Are you happy now, you jerk," Ches glared at his friend. "That girl's so confused she doesn't know what to do."

"Well, that's not our problem," Trey replied.

Ches was shocked by his friend's response. "That's not like you, Trey."

"Well, what the hell are you gonna' do with a girl that turns into a black widow spider, Ches?" His voice had reached another octave. "You have no idea what you're thinking. And, dressing her in Tricia's clothes! What the hell's that all about? She needs to be with someone like herself. She needs to be with Evan; and, now he's gone!" Trey grabbed another piece of bacon. "Man, this is good."

Ches was upon him in three strides. His fist cracked against Trey's jaw sending the piece of bacon flying from his hand and onto the floor.

Trey caught himself before he stumbled backward into the kitchen table. A trickle of blood ran from the corner of his mouth and he wiped it with the back of his hand. Then, he turned to see the bacon lying on the linoleum floor. "Awe man, that was good bacon." Trey quickly grabbed the plate of bacon, opened the oven door and carefully set the plate inside. "We'll want this later." He then warily grinned. "Okay, Ches. It's my turn."

Ches planted his feet and motioned his friend forward. "Alrighty, bring it on." Trey was quick; however, Ches had endurance and strength.

Trey immediately spun and landed a barefoot alongside Ches's face. Ches stumbled backward and slammed into the table. It tipped and several plates crashed to the floor. Trey rolled his eyes. "You donkey's hind-end. I just bought those plates!"

"Awe, quit your whining. You got those at a garage-sale."

"Why you inconsiderate...!" Trey charged Ches and wrestled him to the kitchen floor. Ches quickly rolled and had Trey in a head lock.

Hearing the ruckus, Lana appeared from the bedroom and stood just a few feet away. Her mouth hung open in shock as she glanced around at the broken dishes lying about the floor and the two engaged in a brawl. "Oh, my gosh! What are you doing?"

Ches glanced up at her; he grimaced. "Fighting.

Trey here needs a lesson in manners." His thick arm squeezed tightly around his friend's throat.

"Don't! You're hurting him!" Lana cried.

Trey rolled his eyes. "No, sweetheart, he isn't hurting me," he choked out. "We fight like this all the time."

"You gonna' be nice?" Ches breathed into his face.

Trey's eyes became narrowed slits and he didn't answer. Ches released him anyway and Trey stood. He then brushed himself off, ran a hand through his hair, then bent to pick up the broken pieces of glass. Lana quickly bent beside him and helped.

"I don't need your help." Trey remarked.

Lana quietly continued to pick up the pieces of broken glass. Tension lay as a thick cloud within the small kitchen and neither spoke.

Lana took a breath then stated, "I'm sorry I'm causing you all these problems." She didn't meet Trey's stare. "And, I'll leave as soon as I'm done helping." She glanced down at the clothing she was wearing—Tricia's clothes. She had heard Trey's objection to her wearing them, and briefly wondered who Tricia was. Then, she apologized again. "I'm sorry, but I don't know what else to wear." She stood to her feet and dropped the broken glass in the wooden trash bin; it thundered against the wooden bottom.

Ches remained quiet as he leaned against the counter

with his arms crossed and observed.

Trey grabbed a broom and quickly swept the tiny fragments of glass into a dustpan. Then, he discarded them into the trash bin. He needed some time to mull over the clothing issue.

Lana headed toward the bedroom, but then suddenly turned and stated, "I do need to thank you both for helping me though. Thank you." Suddenly feeling awkward, she again quickly disappeared into the bedroom.

Trey could feel Ches's eyes boring into his back. He sighed heavily then regretfully announced, "It's time to eat. Call her out here."

"So, does that mean she can stay?" Ches asked.

"No; not exactly. It just means that I need some time to think about things. Plus, my jaw hurts, which means it'll take a little longer."

Ches grabbed three new plates from the cupboard. "Well then, *you* go and get her."

Trey scowled, thought about the situation for a moment, then picked up his ball cap from the counter and placed it on his head. In three quick strides, he was in front of the bedroom door knocking. "Lana, may I come in? I promise I won't bite." He tossed a wink and crooked smirk at Ches. Ches eyed him suspiciously.

A small *yes* came from inside the bedroom as she

unlocked the door. Trey's grin was tight lipped. He stepped inside, closed the door behind him and locked it.

Ches was there in three long strides, listening through the wood.

Lana sat down on the bed and folded her hands on her lap. She fidgeted nervously as Trey sat down next to her.

"Lana," he slowly began as he struggled for the right words. "I...this whole situation isn't...good. It's not that I have anything against you—who could?" He leaned slightly away from her and glanced her up and down. "I mean, look at you: you're a gorgeous girl; you're kind and considerate; *and*, you've lost your parents, which I'm truly sorry about." His look was sincere; he continued. "Then, there's this spider thing; I don't even *know* what to say about that." His brows knitted together above his bright blue eyes and his face scrunched up in uncertainty. He was quiet for a moment, seeming to be collecting his thoughts.

Lana glanced at him then at her own hands wringing in her lap. She wasn't quite sure what to say. The remembrance of her parent's camper lying in the mountain valley was excruciatingly painful. She immediately shoved the memory to the back of her mind to suppress it—either that or she would begin crying, then, she would have to deal with transforming into that horrible creature yet again. She took a deep breath. That would be the trick—remain in control. Her feelings suddenly pounded upon her like water from an ruptured dam. Tears brimmed in her wide brown eyes and she suddenly began to sob.

"Oh geesh. What did I do?" Trey got to his feet. I didn't mean to make you cry."

Ches banged on the door. "Trey, what's going on in there? Is Lana crying?"

"Yeah," Trey answered slightly annoyed. "It wasn't intentional."

"Trey, you're so full of crap. Now, open this door."

Trey obeyed. It wasn't that he feared Ches. It was just that Ches was slightly older than he, by three months, and was more like an older brother: and, sparring with him once a day was enough. His jaw still hurt.

Ches rushed in through the door. His eyes raced around the room and paused on Lana. Her face was hidden in her hands and she was crying. "You moron. What did you do?" His irate glance raced to Trey. "You'll cause her to transform, you idiot."

Trey tossed his hands in the air in innocence. "I swear; I didn't do anything. In fact, I was complimenting her and apologizing for her loss."

Ches pushed past him and sat next to Lana on the

bed. He immediately gathered her in his arms. "It's okay. It's okay," he whispered into her ear. He gently stroked her hair as tears streamed along his shirt and dampened his chest. Then, he lightly pressed his hands against her back, feeling for anything that might be pushing through or tearing through the skin—nothing yet. He sighed in relief. Her slender body trembled against his and he gently rubbed his hands along the silky material in the attempt to calm her. "I'm sorry Trey's such an idiot," he whispered.

"Hey, I heard that." Trey scowled. He suddenly felt uncomfortable. "I'll go check on the food."

"Lana, are you going to be okay? I didn't feel anything coming from your back." Ches smiled crookedly.

"That's good," she mumbled. She hurriedly slipped her hand beneath her shirt and touched the hour-glass mark next to her navel. Nothing. "And, there's no webbing." She added as she grinned half-heartedly. "I wonder why nothing's happening; why I'm not changing."

Ches looked into her eyes and their gaze momentarily locked. The desire to kiss her was overwhelming—saturating every fiber of his being. He struggled against taking her in his arms and kissing her cherry colored lips, then her cheeks, then her eyelids, every crevice of her neck.

Lana blinked her eyes and he pulled her close; his lips barely brushed her cheek as he answered, "Well, that's a good thing—right? Maybe, I can help you after all." They sat in silence for a moment. Then Ches asked, "Would you like something to eat?"

Lana's head still swam, like vegetables in soup. She thought of her parents and her brother; and, now, she thought of the person before her. *Concentrate on your breathing*, she thought. *Take slow, deep breaths. Think about the aroma of cooking food, eggs and bacon.* She buried her face within the nape of Ches's shoulder. The smell of his clothing was fresh, invigorating; and his body emanated a blend of soap and cologne. She began to relax slightly, draw on the warming comfort of his embrace, the soft soothing words he continued to console her with, and the scent of his body.

Slowly, Lana nodded her head; she had suddenly become famished.

Ches had given Lana various things to eat since she had first arrived: fruit, toast, a slice of pizza. However, it had been days since she had eaten an entire meal. And, with the trauma her body had experienced and the pain and conflict she was feeling because of Evan, she had mostly slept.

Her mouth watered as she picked up the fork and

began to eat and the urge to tear into the eggs, bacon and toast was overwhelming; it took an immense amount of effort to restrain herself. Yet, the urge to grab the raw pieces of bacon still cooking in the oven, or to eat the eggs right from the carton sitting on the counter, was even worse. She couldn't understand what was happening to her. She needed to find Evan and talk to him, question him at length. However, she knew he was angry, angry about her and Ches.

It wasn't fair, she thought. *I didn't do anything. Ches didn't do anything. He was just trying to comfort me while I was upset. Evan, what's the matter with you?* She wanted to scream it, shout the words at him and tell him how stupid he was acting. She was angry with him for his faulty assumption, yet she ached to be with him, ached terribly to the point that every crevice of her body hurt and her heart felt as if it had cracked. Suddenly, she laid down the toast she was eating and placed her hands to her chest. It hurt, hurt deeply. She was glad she had never gotten involved with anyone before if this was what love was like. She wanted to curse.

"Lana?" Ches touched her arm and her thoughts reverted back to where she was. She suddenly became aware of him and Trey staring at her as she had been clutching at her chest. Her face flushed several shades of pink. "Are you in pain?"

Trey had just shoveled a fork full of eggs into his mouth followed by a bite of buttered toast. He eyed her suspiciously. "What were you thinking about?" he asked while chewing.

"Nothing," she answered too quickly; the pink of her face spread to her neck and chest.

"Well then, let me ask you this"—

Ches shot Trey a warning look while Lana's face had frozen.

"What are you going to do now?" Trey asked. "Apparently you've upset your friend; and, out of any of us, he's the only one who can associate with your..." He placed his fingers in the air and made several small movements, representing quotation marks, "...little problem."

Lana glanced down at the few remaining items on her plate: the deliciously cooked bacon, an egg brimming with yolk and a half eaten piece of toast. Nearly a minute had passed as the kitchen clock clicked away the seconds. Trey had mentally counted them down in his head, fifty-five seconds.

"I don't know," she finally answered. "If Evan doesn't help me, I don't know what I'll do."

Trey's gaze shot to Ches whose face remained expressionless. Trey then nodded his head in finality and raised a crooked brow.

His *I told you so* attitude raised the hairs on the back of Ches's neck. Ches suddenly shoved his chair away from the table; the glass plates rattled and a fork sailed to the floor. Lana flinched.

"All right, Trey, I get the message." He then looked at Lana with pain vivid in his azure-colored eyes. "As soon as you've finished eating, I'll take you to find him." The thought of losing her ruined the remaining taste of breakfast in his mouth; he grimaced.

Lana grinned half-heartedly as she stared down at her food. "I'm not sure how to get to the cabin; *and*, I don't even know if he'll speak to me." Her fork poked at the thin white layer of egg and they all watched as the bright yellow goo ran onto her plate. "Ches," Lana looked into his eyes; the wounding behind them was unmistakable. "I also didn't tell you. My brother, Samuel, is missing…" for a moment she was quiet "…and, he was also bitten."

Chapter 25

Spence occasionally glanced over at Booger, Marty and Colette who sat in the living room observing him as he excitedly paced back and forth. He tapped his forehead often and muttered words like: spider, transform, and power, beneath his breath. Marty and Booger's mouths were open and their eyes were wide as they watched every step and movement Spence made. He had ordered them to remain quiet, cease their exuberant chattering while he contemplated the situation.

Colette sat with her legs crossed nonchalantly smoking a cigarette. She curiously studied the gray ash as it grew longer and longer, wondering as to how long it would get before falling off or being quickly tapped into the ashtray.

"Colette, are you paying attention?" Spence suddenly halted in his tracks. "This is important! More important than anything!" He walked over, snatched the half burned cigarette out of her hand and ground it out in the overflowing ashtray. "Now, pay attention!"

The ashes landed in her lap. "Hey!" Her face twisted unnaturally and she suddenly became irate. "Whaddya do that for? You're not doing anythin' but adding to the dirt trail in your carpet." She stood and angrily brushed them to the floor then coughed. "You looked pretty pathetic as a spider when I saw ya'. Heck, you could barely drag yourself across the yard."

"Don't you understand?" Spence retorted. "This is the biggest thing ever! I can now transform into a *spider*—a black widow spider—and the power and intensity are phenomenal! It's amazing!" He threw his hands in the air. "And, I was hit by a tractor trailer, you stupid twit! A tractor trailer! And, I'm still standing here to tell about it. That's why I was dragging myself across the yard!"

"So, what can you do with this power, Spence?" Marty eagerly asked as he awkwardly sat forward on the edge of the couch. The entire left side of him, from his neck to his chest, was bulging with bandages and his left arm was in a cast.

"Yeah...Sp...Spence," Booger asked excitedly, "wha...what...c...can...you...do?"

Spence's eyes grew wild and a demented grin spread across his face. "You have no idea, do you? I can scale a wall in a matter of seconds, run as fast as almost any car, and crush a bowling ball within my grip. Plus, when I'm in that form, my auditory senses are heightened to an astronomical level by the tiny hairs that cover my legs, *and*, I can see so far! It's incredible!"

"Well, Sp...Spence," Booger stuttered, how...how...did...you become...a...sp... spider?"

Spence's rust-colored brows creased. "That's a darn good question, Booger. I'm tryin' ta' figure that one out myself."

"Well, *I* was bitten by that horrible looking creature and I have the injury right here to prove it." Marty gently patted the bandage encasing his shoulder. "Will I change into a spider too?" His weary voice contained a slight hint of excitement while the proposal of being a black widow was fearful, yet also enthralling.

"I...don't...wanna...be...a...black...widow...spider...Spence," Booger interjected. "That...girl...didn't...look...strong...or...or...fast."

Spence walked over to Booger and laid his hand on Booger's shoulder. "Booger, I'm almost certain it's because she was weak and didn't know how to use that power. The instant I changed, I could feel the strength surging through me, the anger and rage. Some mealy-mouthed girl isn't going to be able to control that. She's probably some *mama's brat*. But, as far as what made *me* change, I'm gonna' hav'ta think about that." Spence began to pace again as various thoughts raced through his mind.

"Well, weren't both you and Marty bitten by the same creature?" Colette asked.

Spence stopped dead in his tracks; his expression was set as he looked at her. "You have a good point."

"But, I didn't feel any energy or power when I was bitten," Marty stated. "In fact, it was the opposite. It hurt like hell! I thought I was dying."

"The floor creaked as Spence began pacing again and he mumbled to himself. "So, if you're bitten you don't automatically change; but, I was bitten and I changed immediately. Hmm; this is interesting." His thoughts scurried through the many events that had occurred throughout the past few days.

He paused briefly on the more valued of occasions, like when he had pulled Lana from the water and had tasted the blood that ran along her cheek. He had been sadly disappointed to find that it tasted ordinary, like blood.

Thoughts of the mesmeric moments spent in the back room where he had relished in her pain as he examined and butchered a few of her black widow limbs, focused in his mind. Now, *that* had been exhilarating. He had kissed her once then, swallowing her cries as she screamed out in pain. Fresh blood was upon her lips and he had also tasted it then. The taste seemed slightly different though, more refreshing and invigorating, and afterwards, he desired it more than anything, as if he needed it to survive. A thought suddenly occurred to him and he spun around to face Colette.

"Colette…" He eyed her closely. "Did you by chance taste any blood on my lips when you kissed me?"

She searched her mind for a moment then answered, "No."

Spence then addressed all three. "Did *any* of you get *any* of *her or the male's blood* on you besides me?"

"I did," Marty quickly volunteered. "When I was fighting with the male I did, but I didn't change."

"No…no…not…me," Booger shook his head.

They all then turned toward Colette. Silence filled the room as they waited for her to answer. Meanwhile, she had lit another cigarette and was again challenging the ash to a match of wits.

"*Well?*" Spence pressed. "Did you get blood on you or not?"

Colette quickly tapped the long ash into the ashtray then she answered, "Yes, I did; I tasted her blood like the deer you shoot and are about to slaughter. And, it was good, so I tasted it more than once. There!" She crossed her legs defiantly. "So, sue me."

Spence grinned.

Another hour of debating passed and the four came to the probable conclusion that the only way Spence had been able to become a black widow was by tasting Lana's blood. The only question remaining was whether or not Colette could change.

"But I don't wanna' be a spider, Spence," Colette also complained. "Those things are gross."

"Oh, quit your whinin', Colette. Ya' wanna' be useful to me; don't ya'? Then, you'll do what I ask." He kissed her on her ruby lips and led her outside.

Chapter 26

The jeep roared to life and Ches shoved the gear shifter into reverse. The top was off and he glanced over to make certain Lana was buckled in. Then, he looked up at Trey who was standing at the entrance to the house. Trey nodded his head at his good friend, reassuring him that he was doing the right thing; however, Ches's rigid expression was unchanging as the engine snarled and he irritably backed out of the garage. Punching the shifter into first gear, he pressed the gas and steered the vehicle toward the main road. He thought he might know where the cabin was according to Lana's description—located on 200 acres of land outside the town of Billet.

The sun's rays reflected off the shiny chrome and the glossy black paint: they warmed Lana's skin. She sat quietly; her hands folded on her lap. Her stomach fluttered nervously like a cluster of butterflies trapped in a net. The road sped by and her fingers clutched at the skirt she was wearing—Tricia's skirt. And, though the top was made of the finest silk and the skirt of the softest cotton, they began to feel itchy against her skin. She suddenly wanted to change.

"Ches?" she asked cautiously, "who was Tricia?"

He glanced at her out of the corner of his eye; then he stared at the road ahead. His countenance looked as if it was carved of stone. Lana turned her head; the clusters of trees and few houses she watched whizzing by were her only refuge from the discomforting silence.

Ches downshifted and turned a sharp curve; they could see the Hobbs' estate gates just ahead. He suddenly pulled to the side of the road, shut the motor off and turned in his seat to face Lana. The ache was still apparent in his stricken face as he spoke. "Tricia was my girlfriend; she was everything to me."

"And Trey?" Lana fidgeted with the skirt.

"Tricia was Trey's sister."

"Oh no," Lana breathed. "No wonder he was so upset about the clothes."

"I guess it's understandable," Ches explained. "She was the only family he had." He looked over at Lana through paining eyes while forcing himself to focus on the skirt. Then, he continued. "Their parents were killed in a car accident when Tricia and he were younger. Anyway, after Tricia died in the boating accident, we both picked various things in remembrance of her, then Trey gave the rest of her clothing and things to the church."

Ches was quiet for a moment as he rubbed his hands

over the black leather steering wheel. He then glanced up to look into Lana's eyes. "That was one of my favorite outfits she wore." He gently touched Lana's shoulder and fingered the silky material between his forefinger and thumb. "But, now you're here and that helps...me anyway," he added.

Lana looked into his eyes; they were the deepest shade of blue, a sea of emotion. He was kind and generous, and gorgeous beyond all rights.

"I don't want you to leave." He leaned across the seat toward her and his large, firm body pressed against hers. Lana could feel his heart beating through his button-down shirt. She closed her eyes.

Ches's warm breath was upon her face and the mild scent of the soap he used wafted from his body and lightly drifted into her nostrils. He cupped her petite form within his muscular arms and gently embraced her. His mouth was now inches from hers. She could feel the gentle wisps of his soft words against her lips. They moved from her lips and disappeared into her hair. Her body shivered slightly as they then slipped warmly within her ear.

"Lana, stay with me. Please."

Lana's heart was pounding wildly and the butterflies she had felt earlier had become frantic in the attempts to break free. Her feelings for Ches were mixed, confusing.

It was unlike the way she felt for Evan; her heart ached when she thought of Evan and every fiber of her being longed to be with him, be a part of him. Her head was spinning in circles and for a moment she was lost—lost in the passionate embrace of this person who wanted and needed her, but still lost in the desire for the one *she* needed and wanted. For some odd reason she wanted to laugh or possibly cry; however, something caught her attention and she stiffened. The odor of Spence's arachnid blood was suddenly flooding her nose. It made her feel sick. She had been so distracted by Ches's tender advances that she hadn't sensed anything out of the ordinary, especially danger.

"Ches," she stated with slight urgency.

"What is it?" he immediately asked as he felt her body stiffen.

Two enormous black widow spiders were crouched in front of the jeep; Marty and Booger stood at the vehicle's rear. They were surrounded.

"We've come for the girl!" Marty suddenly shouted.

The saga continues in…

Spidey Legs Lana
Black Widow
Book 2

Check out Tessa LaRock's other releases….

Breinigsville, PA USA
01 December 2009

228381BV00002B/2/P